"Are you always so—so ruthless?"

"Always," he confirmed. But added when she just stood and silently stared at him, "Though I can be quite cute sometimes."

She laughed. And Nyall grinned. Then, standing away from his car, he stretched out his hands to her shoulders and, holding her, bent down and gently kissed her lightly parted lips.

"You're pretty cute yourself, come to think of it," he murmured.

Dear Reader,

Help us celebrate life, love and happy-ever-afters with our great new series.

Everybody loves a party and birthday parties best of all, so join some of your favorite authors and celebrate in style with seven fantastic new romances. One for every day of the week, in fact, and each featuring a truly wonderful woman whose story fits the lines of the old rhyme "Monday's child is..."

> *Monday's child is fair of face*
> *Tuesday's child is full of grace,*
> *Wednesday's child is full of woe,*
> *Thursday's child has far to go,*
> *Friday's child is loving and giving,*
> *Saturday's child works hard for its living,*
> *And a child that's born on a Sunday*
> *Is bonny and blithe and good and gay.*

(Anon.)

Does the day that you're born on affect your character? Some people think so—if you want to find out more, read our exciting new series. Available wherever Harlequin books are sold:

Happy reading,

The Editors, Harlequin Romance

The Marriage Business
Jessica Steele

Harlequin Books

TORONTO • NEW YORK • LONDON
AMSTERDAM • PARIS • SYDNEY • HAMBURG
STOCKHOLM • ATHENS • TOKYO • MILAN
MADRID • WARSAW • BUDAPEST • AUCKLAND

ISBN 0-373-03407-5

THE MARRIAGE BUSINESS

First North American Publication 1996.

Copyright © 1995 by Jessica Steele.

CHAPTER ONE

AVENA ALLADICE paused in brushing her long rich golden-coloured hair and owned that she was just a tiny bit out of sorts that morning. She looked at her reflection in the dressing-table mirror and, as large eyes of a brilliant blue stared back at her, was a mite ashamed that she could be in any way unhappy with her lot. Her complexion was milky white with just a hint of the palest pink in her cheeks. She came from a long line of beautiful women, and according to her grandmother she was the most beautiful of them all—but then, her grandmother was biased.

Avena suddenly became aware of the minutes ticking by. She brushed her hair back from her face and, with a few deft movements, expertly flicked it into a chignon—the style she always adopted for the office.

That morning, however, she was not going to do very much in her office but was going to the opening of Oakby Trading's new headquarters. Oakby Trading came under the umbrella of the multi-million pound conglomerate Lancaster Holdings and the firm she worked for, Marton Exclusives, was exceedingly anxious to do business with any company connected with Lancasters.

Marton Exclusives, a firm which manufactured high-class sports equipment, was owned by her brothers-in-law, Tony and Martin—the name meant to be more an abbreviation of 'Marathon' than of

Martin and Tony. Avena was their finance director and had done well since she had first gone to work for them. The term nepotism, however, did not apply. She had laboured hard in the six years she had been with them, soaking up figure work like a sponge, and she knew that neither Tony nor Martin would have promoted her if she had not been up to it.

They did not come much harder-headed than her two brothers-in-law—which made it just as well that neither of her elder sisters, Lucille and Coral, was a shrinking violet.

'They take after your mother,' her grandmother had told her once when, at fifteen years old, she had been amazed at the anger in both her sisters when their husbands had suggested that they spend less so that they could keep more in the firm's coffers. 'You, on the other hand, given that you get your looks from the female side, are all your father.'

'Are you saying that my mother married Daddy for his money?' She had been horrified at the idea.

'Ah!' Her grandmother had paused. 'I must have forgotten what an intelligent child you are.' And, in that, Avena had her answer though Grandmother Carstairs, her mother's mother, had quickly taken her mind away from that shocking news to tell her, 'Your father was a gentleman.'

'Was he?' Avena had asked, eager to hear more about her father who had died when she was ten.

Over the next year, however, she had seen evidence for herself that her mother and both her sisters were motivated by a love of money, when the fortunes of Marton Exclusives had come near the brink of bankruptcy. That was when her mother had declared that she would have helped them out if she could, but that the amount her husband had left her had dwindled to practically nothing.

And while Avena had observed that, 'penniless', her mother did not seem to be changing her lifestyle any— still living in gown shops and spending just as before— her two sisters were talking not of doing all they could to help but, astonishingly, talking in terms of dumping their respective husbands if matters didn't improve!

'But . . . you've both got brains; why don't you go out and get jobs? It would all help!' she had protested. Neither of her sisters wanted children but plainly not because they were career-minded.

Lucille had looked at her as if she were mad. But it had been Coral who had replied, '*You* go and get a job. If you're so high-minded about it, you *go* and get a job instead of living off Mother all the time!'

That had shaken Avena. She had never thought that she had been living off her mother, but with the latter talking of having very little left she had begun to question whether she should stay on at school the extra year as she had intended.

Instinctively she had wanted to ask her grandmother, but after having moved in with them six years ago to be what help she could when her daughter's husband had died her grandmother had rowed once too often and once too angrily with her daughter a month before, and had moved out. Besides which, she had realised, although Grandmother Carstairs tried hard not to have favourites, Avena could not but know that, as her grandmother was special to her, she was special to her grandmother.

On the grounds that her grandmother would from the love she had for her make sure she stayed on at school and would insist, since she achieved top grades, that she go on to university, Avena had realised she could not ask her advice. Instead, after thinking matters over very carefully—not to mention discovering that she had a pride that was up in arms at having Coral turn the tables on her in the way that she had—Avena had approached her brothers-in-law.

Tony and Martin had been business partners before Tony had met Lucille and subsequently introduced Martin to her sister Coral. Her two sisters had married in the same year. They had all been together at one of her mother's dinner parties when, her sisters having gone upstairs with their mother to complain that their well-to-do husbands were going through a second rocky financial patch, Avena had found herself alone with the two business partners. 'I need a job,' she had blurted out. 'You haven't got anything in the clerical line, have you?'

'An Alladice working?' Tony had enquired sarcastically. But, while she'd coloured up, Martin—the marginally less sharp of the two—had explained that they had paperwork by the ton but couldn't afford to pay her very much.

'I wouldn't want very much—just enough to keep me in the occasional pair of shoes—that sort of thing.'

Tony had looked at her seriously. 'Well, provided you don't buy your shoes from the same expensive source as your sister...'

A month later, her parent making not the smallest protest, she had started work at Marton Exclusives. There had been a mountain of paperwork and Avena, having a quick brain, had shifted it. In fact, she had found that she had an aptitude for it and, once she knew what she was doing, had moved the paperwork very quickly.

She had been working at Marton Exclusives six months when the firm had begun to recover from its set-back and she had been put on a realistic salary. And six months later, as the firm had gone from strength to strength and after a few incidents when she could have explained to her sisters more about the firm's finances but hadn't, the two partners had realised that her loyalty to the firm was in a separate compartment from the loyalty she had for her sisters.

Over the next few years she had attended evening classes, read and absorbed everything she could about the financial running of a company. And, as her brothers-in-law had discovered how easily she coped with spreadsheets and how at home she was with matters financial, she had assumed, and been given, more and more responsibility. So that, as time had gone on and the firm had become yet more buoyant, the three of them had found that she had been doing the work of financial director for twelve months before their bank manager had referred to her as such. From that day the two partners had conferred the title on her.

Which was fine, Avena thought as she left her dressing-table and donned the crisp pale green two-piece she was going to wear on what looked like being a warm summer's day. So why did she feel as if she was missing something? She had a good job, a good home, a super grandmother a couple of hours' motoring away in Worcestershire—what more could she want?

Feeling impatient with herself, she left her room and, aware of the inadvisability of looking into her mother's room to say goodbye, tripped lightly down the stairs of the large, rambling house she had been brought up in, and headed for the kitchen.

'Good morning, Mrs Parsons,' she greeted their housekeeper of the last six months—housekeepers never stayed with her mother for very long. She went over to the coffee-percolator and poured herself a cup. 'Any problems you need help with?' she enquired with a smile. She liked Mrs Parsons and was hopeful that she would stay longer than her predecessors.

'If you don't mind me saying, I think you should have a proper breakfast,' seemed to be the housekeeper's only complaint.

'Tomorrow I will,' Avena promised, having a slender but curvy figure with never the smallest need to diet. 'Scrambled eggs with toast?' she suggested, and felt quite cheered when that lady smiled.

'In the breakfast-room?'

Clearly Mrs Parsons liked matters in their correct order. 'If you insist,' she laughed, saw Mrs Parson's smile become a grin and, because she was meeting up with her brothers-in-law, made her goodbyes and went out to her car.

She had saved hard to buy her car, yet it had seemed a tremendous amount of money to spend in one go. She had asked her grandmother's opinion.

'Blow it!' had been her advice.

'All of it?' Earning money and saving hard had taught her the value of it.

'All of it,' Grandmother Carstairs had decreed. 'With your looks some man will soon snap you up. He'll have money and——'

Avena's shocked expression had caused her to break off. 'Gran!' Her mother had married for money—her marriage had been a disaster. Her sisters had married for the same reason and their marriages were pretty similar—and had nearly been over when their husbands' finances had rocked that particular time. 'I couldn't marry for money!' she'd exclaimed fervently, and had known it for a fact.

'Don't I know that?' her grandmother had smiled. 'Don't I know that you're as unlike your sisters—your mother too for that matter—as chalk is from cheese? But it stands to reason that if he hasn't already got money, then to gain you your future husband will work his fingers to the bone to give you everything you'll ever want.'

'Did I ever tell you that you wear glasses that are a wee bit rose-tinted in my favour?' Avena had laughed fondly.

Her grandmother had laughed too. Though she'd added, with an oblique reference to the pleasant but unthreatening types whom her youngest granddaughter associated with, 'You're not afraid of meeting *real* men, are you, love?'

Avena had shaken her head. She had occasionally dated other types—men like Tony and Martin. But she had found them brash and insensitive, interested only in being seen with her, in making conquests. If they were 'real' men she would prefer safe, if dull types. Yet safe, dull types seemed to be vulnerable somehow—and could be hurt. And, while her sisters exulted in their power to hurt, such power as bestowed by the Alladice beauty alarmed her.

Which, with her position of financial director for an ever expanding firm meaning that she had to work long hours, curtailed the time she had available for dating—a situation she was not too unhappy about. She supposed she would quite like to marry one day, but never for money like Coral and Lucille, who, appallingly, had affairs to brighten up their inconsequential lives.

She stopped her car at the bottom of the drive and, about to get out to open the wooden gates, saw that the paper-boy had arrived and had started to do that chore for her.

'Why, thank you, James,' she smiled, getting out of her car anyway and coming to assist with the other gate. 'I'll return the favour for you one day.'

He went a trace pink and Avena, aware that the fifteen-year-old might be having problems with his adolescence, was all sensitivity when he suggested gruffly, 'You could do me one big favour anyway, if you like.'

'Name it,' she invited with an encouraging smile.

'I'm playing the accordion in the village concert in a couple of weeks—can you come?'

She had seen the advertisement about the concert pinned to a telegraph pole when she had been out walking. 'Count me in,' she accepted. 'Do I pay you for my ticket?'

'You can pay at the door of the village hall,' he beamed, and, jumping on his cycle, he went pell-mell up the drive.

It was a glorious morning, and whenever possible Avena put her foot down and sped to her office.

'I don't have to tell you how important today is,' Tony addressed her in heavy tones, a few minutes before they were due to set off for the opening of the new Oakby Trading headquarters.

'You're not expecting to do business today, surely?' she enquired. She knew that Tony and Martin were keen to expand yet further, but to her mind everyone would be more interested in champagne and publicity—unlike Marton Exclusives, which would be holding an open day in six weeks' time with business very much in mind.

'We did very well to get an invitation—I've been trying to get in with Oakby Trading for a year,' Tony replied. 'We can't afford to let the grass grow now—if there's so much as a sniff of a chance of doing business, I want to be in there.'

Tony had insisted that she must go with them to the opening, and she had been flattered that they wanted her with them, but now she was beginning to wonder. 'Just why *am* I coming along?' she asked in her usual forthright manner. She glanced at Martin, who was starting to look a shade uncomfortable.

'You're an asset to any firm,' he mumbled. 'We're bound to get noticed with you with——'

The hint of mutiny that started to come to her face caused Tony to interrupt—fast. 'It's nothing like that,' he contradicted, with an impatient look to Martin. 'It's just that should we get the chance to talk business, *should* we get asked if we can afford materials to pay for any colossal order which Oakby Trading may consider putting our way, you'll be on the spot—with your usual honesty—to tell them it'd be no problem, and anything else in connection with finance.'

She wasn't quite sure that she trusted his reply but since he knew full well that there was positively no way that she would be used, or would make capital out of the looks she had inherited, she had, for the moment, to go along with it. It was true, she would be able to answer any questions about finance relating to an order and she knew, with Tony referring to her honesty, that in the years she had been in charge of finance Marton Exclusives had acquired a name for straight dealing; she liked to think that she had contributed to that.

They went in Tony's car and the opening of the new Oakby Trading headquarters went with a swing. Avena renewed acquaintance with many people, most of whom she liked, some she was not too keen on.

'Your switchboard blocked a call I tried to get put through to you the other day,' one earnest type whose name she was trying desperately hard to remember buttonholed her to complain.

'I was probably out,' she replied tactfully; it was not unknown for her to request that none but urgent calls be put through if she was busy. She added, smiling, 'I hope they were able to put you through to someone who could deal with your query.'

'I didn't want to be put through to anybody else,' he replied. Oh, dear, here it comes, she thought. 'I rang hoping to ask you to have dinner with me.'

There was no easy way of doing this. She'd had to do it before, but it never got any easier. 'I'm sorry,' she replied, sensitive, smiling gently, 'but I make it a rule never to mix business with pleasure.'

'It wasn't business I want to see you about. I——'

'I'm sorry,' she repeated, and was forced to bring out her 'I'm not available' phrase, which less painfully conveyed most times that she was going steady with someone.

Thankfully, at that moment, two other men came up to chat, and although she made a point of including the other man, whose name she just then remembered was Robert, she also made sure that she didn't give him a chance to ask her out again.

For the next hour she chatted and sipped and chatted and nibbled, but couldn't see a sign of anyone from Oakby Trading rushing up to enquire pantingly into their credit viability.

She looked around for either Martin or Tony. This kind of do could go on all day. Were they, ever hopeful of an order, really going to stick it out to the end?

She thought of the work she could be doing and, catching sight of Tony in conversation with a couple of men, wondered how he would view it if she went over and told him that, the courtesies observed, she was taking a taxi back to the office. Then she remembered that he wanted her on the spot in case there was the smallest sniff of a chance of their picking up some business—even the smallest order would give them a foot in the door with Oakby's.

For another half-hour she circulated, was waylaid, chatted, nibbled, smilingly refusing another drink. She had been waylaid by a couple of here-I-am-girls-come-and-get-me types and was on the brink of using her 'I'm not available' tactic, when a man who had been in the same study group as herself at evening classes some years ago came over and joined them.

'Walter!' she exclaimed in pleasure. Walter was a happily married family man who in those days had forever made her laugh.

'As I live and breathe, Avena Alladice—the only other woman I'd leave home for!' he exclaimed, and, like the big bear he was, he caught hold of her and gave her a hug and a peck on the cheek.

'How are you getting on? I lost sight of you when we passed our exams. How...?' And as Avena introduced the other men there followed a happy never-time-to-draw-breath question-and-answer session.

Walter was as witty and capable as ever of making her laugh. He did so then when he soberly requested that she call him Walt as it was better for his image. Then as she laughed and turned her head so her eyes caught sight of a tall, immaculately suited, dark-haired man standing there, his eyes on her, and all laughter died on her lips. The man was around thirty-five and had an air about him that just screamed VIP—not to mention the fact that the man she had been introduced to as the general manager of Oakby Trading was standing next to him in respectful conversation.

'So—er—how are the family?' she asked Walter, and for once in her life found she was having difficulty getting her thoughts together. Grief, she didn't know the VIP from Adam yet he was sending her brain patterns haywire. Somehow, she knew at that very moment that here was a man to avoid.

She wanted to look at him again. While the other men attempted to look interested as Walter began to tell her how his little ones were now quite big ones, she felt a desperate urge to take a look at the newcomer once more. For newcomer he was. Had he been there before then without question she would have seen him. With certainty, she just knew it would have been impossible for the man to have been in the same room and her not to have known it.

She told herself not to be so ridiculous as conversation became general. Then the manager of Oakby Trading came into her line of vision. She watched him as he went over and had a word with Tony. She saw Tony smile, look pleased—delighted wasn't overstating it—then saw how he went and rounded up Martin. Were they leaving? She hoped so; she was feeling most definitely—strangely—unnerved.

'Has any lucky male managed to ensnare you yet?' Walter asked with a glance down to her left hand, perhaps remembering that those who'd chanced their arm at college had soon discovered that she was minded to work, not play.

Avena did not get the chance to answer for just then Tony and Martin came up to them. 'Could we have a word?' Martin asked.

'This is Walter . . .' She began to introduce him and the other two.

'*Now!*' Tony said pointedly.

'We'll have a chat later.' Walter took the unveiled hint, and, taking hold of her hand, gallantly kissed it before, unruffled, unoffended, he and the other two men ambled away.

'Did you have to be so rude?' Avena remonstrated, unable to think of anything in this party atmosphere that warranted her immediate attention; she refused to believe that anyone at such a function had asked Tony to open his order-book.

'Nyall Lancaster wants to meet us!' Tony stated without further ado.

'Nyall Lancaster!' she echoed.

'He just heads Lancaster Holdings, that's all,' Martin slipped in quietly, looking a touch overawed.

Avena knew that a Nyall Lancaster headed Lancaster Holdings, just as she knew that the immaculately suited, dark-haired man she had seen looking at her a few minutes ago could be none other than he. 'What does he want to meet us for?' she wanted to know, every instinct alert.

'How the hell should I know?' Tony hissed. 'Just be grateful that, out of all the firms represented here, he wants us to be introduced.'

Her instincts began to quiver. Tony was sharp, intelligent. She knew that he must be aware that there was more to it than that. There were other firms attending that were far more important than Marton's—so the question persisted, why them? And why would a man such as Nyall Lancaster—who had probably only popped in to offer congratulations to his manager—bother anyway?

'Come on,' Tony urged. She did not budge. Was she afraid of the man? Don't be ridiculous! She scoffed at the very idea. 'He's waiting!' Tony seethed.

'You go without me.'

'Don't be an idiot—he wants to meet *you*! Come on, Avena.' Tony changed tone to cajole. 'All you've got to do is be nice to him.'

'Nice to him'! 'He wants to meet *you*'! A feeling of sickness invaded. Visions of her sisters and her mother being 'nice' to men for their own ends nauseated her; Tony was asking her to do the same thing!

Desperately Avena tried to cling on to logic. It was nothing to do with her personally. She was in a working environment. This was work. They could get an order... Logic scoffed at that. Was it likely that a man of Nyall Lancaster's standing would ask to meet *her* and the Marton Exclusives team so he could give them an order? Grief, he dealt in multi-million pound deals. He was a giant whale, they merely tadpoles in the sea of business and, as such, beneath his notice.

'I'd better go and powder my nose.' She fought her way through her congested thoughts.

'Hell's teeth, Avena, we can't keep him waiting!' Tony snapped.

It took all her nerve but she turned her head to look where Nyall Lancaster was in conversation with a couple of other businessmen, and Tony followed her gaze and saw for himself that the head of Lancaster Holdings was not even looking their way, and indeed did not seem to be in any hurry for them to go over.

'I won't be long,' she said, and made her escape.

Her thoughts in the restroom were a quagmire as she battled with anger at the fact that, when she categorically refused to be used, both Tony and Martin cared not a jot so long as they could promote more business. And what about Nyall Lancaster? Who in creation did he think he was that he could say he wanted to meet her, clap his hands and—*voilà*—there she was, delivered?

Fuming, still refusing to be used, Avena strove for calm. She needed to think. Meeting, or rather not meeting but just seeing Nyall Lancaster seemed to have made cool, common-or-garden sense leave her brain. Martin and Tony worked hard for their business, but then so too did she. And nobody had ever told her that she would have to sell herself for the business. Well, maybe sell was overstating it but... She remembered her sisters who didn't appear to give a jot what they had to do when finance was involved. But she wasn't like them.

Nausea started to well up again, and then she remembered. Somewhere in the far reaches of her mind she remembered, recalled, having heard or read somewhere that Nyall Lancaster's reputation for fair dealing was second to none.

A few minutes later Avena reappeared and went out to the front entrance of the building. Good, the commissionaire was still there. She went up to him. 'I wonder, could you get a message to either Mr Martin

Usher or Mr Tony Spicer that Miss Alladice is a little unwell and has gone home?'

The commissionaire, a super man, she thought, assured her that he would pass the message on but first, in view of her being 'indisposed' and because she refused to allow him to escort her to the sick-bay where a nurse could attend to her, insisted on seeing her into a taxi.

By which time Avena felt she didn't know if she was coming or going. What she did feel and know, however, was that having seen Nyall Lancaster—without so much as having said hello to the man—she had never felt so confused, unsettled and altogether mind-blown in her life!

CHAPTER TWO

HER taxi dropped her off at Marton Exclusives but for the first time ever when there was absolutely nothing physically wrong with her Avena went to the car park, got into her car, and took the rest of the day off.

She did not want to go to her office—yet nor did she want to go home. She pointed her car in the direction of Worcestershire. Tomorrow she would work twice as hard and would work late to catch up.

She reached her grandmother's cottage in Kembury in the early afternoon. Her grandmother was not in but Avena had a key and an open invitation to treat the cottage as her own. Realising her grandmother must have gone out to lunch, she let herself in—and was still no clearer as to why she had bolted in the way that she had.

Ten minutes later she sat drinking a cup of tea, and was still trying to come to terms with the effect Nyall Lancaster had had on her—she had shot off as though scalded rather than be introduced to him.

Though on reflection, she pondered, having time now to concentrate her thoughts solely on the way she had reacted, it was not so much Nyall Lancaster she had run away from but Tony and Martin. Perhaps she had over-reacted, but having seen herself being used the way that she had, she concluded that to bolt had been her way of declaring she was not to be used; that she was not like her sisters.

'What a lovely surprise!' her grandmother beamed when half an hour later she halted her beaten-up old Metro on the drive and Avena went out to greet her. 'I recognised your car parked by the kerb, but couldn't believe that on a weekday you'd come to see your old gran.'

There was a question there; Avena was not ready to answer it. 'You, old?' she scoffed, giving her seventy-two-year-old, never-still-a-minute grandmother a hug and a kiss. 'Been out to lunch?' she enquired as they went indoors.

'I've been to book a holiday,' her grandmother replied, and bustled into the kitchen to put the kettle on.

Avena stayed with her for an hour and, having discussed in detail her grandmother's proposed five-week cruise in about six weeks' time, thought she had better think about going home.

'I'd better be going,' she announced with a smile as she took her car keys from her bag—and discovered that her grandmother who loved her so well missed little where she was concerned.

'What's troubling you, love?' she asked gently. 'Is Fergus Bradley still weeping on your shoulder?'

'Oh, Gran, it's not as bad as that!' Fergus Bradley was the recently divorced husband of her friend Kate. He still loved Kate and was having a dreadful time getting over her. 'Anyhow, he's away for a couple of weeks.'

'And giving you a rest. But something's troubling you.'

'You see too much,' Avena laughed, but then confessed, 'I'm a bit off Tony and Martin at the moment.'

'I was never on them,' her grandmother sniffed, and Avena had to laugh. 'Tell them you're leaving— that'll shake them,' she advised.

Avena left Kembury in a much happier frame of mind than when she had arrived. She had never given a thought to giving up her job with Tony and Martin, but it was an idea. The nearer she got to her own home, though, the more she wondered if that option— to hand in her notice—was open to her. After her refusal to be introduced to Nyall Lancaster today—and while Martin might swallow her 'unwell' excuse Tony never would—it could be that the directors of Marton Exclusives had decided that her services were no longer required and that *they* would give her notice.

That was when she realised that the idea of being asked to leave did not bother her one tiny bit, and drew up on the drive of her home to see that her sisters' cars, as they were so frequently, were parked there. She entered the drawing-room knowing that both her sisters were paying her mother a visit.

'Where have you been till now?' Lucille, a brunette—and vivacious when any men were around— just beat her blonde-haired sister, Coral, in demanding aggressively.

Avena looked at the two of them, beautiful both and idle with it. Her glance went on to her equally beautiful mother and she knew that while, apart from hair colouring, they all favoured each other a touch, she had little in common with any of them. 'Hello, Mother,' she courteously greeted her parent, and looked back to Lucille to reply, 'Who says I haven't been to the office?'

'Tony says! He rang me. He's as mad as hell.'

'So's Martin,' Coral chipped in coldly.

'And you care?' Avena tossed at both of them.

'We care when our livelihood's at stake,' Lucille snapped.

'Livelihood'! Grief, she'd only pleaded illness! Nyall Lancaster, if he was anywhere near as fair as he was said to be, would have accepted that and, she thought, remembering the sophisticated man, would by now have forgotten all about it—and her.

'I'll bet you do,' she retorted.

'Why did you do it?' Coral wanted to know.

'It would only have been good manners to have gone and said how do you do when Mr Lancaster had specifically asked to meet you,' her mother, revealing that she knew all about it too, reprimanded her.

They would never understand, any of them. 'I don't think it was me specifically that he wanted to meet——' she began, when Lucille butted in.

'I'd have given my right arm to meet him, yet there you are——'

'All that wealth—and a bachelor into the bargain! Heaven help us, Avena, you want...' Coral interrupted.

But Avena had heard much in the same vein before. Her mother would be butting in at any moment, telling her to buck her ideas up. 'I'm going up to change,' she said, cutting Coral off, and without more ado left the drawing-room and made for the stairs.

She did not go down until after she had heard Lucille and Coral leave. Her mother was dining out and had little to say to her when she went downstairs.

'Have a nice time,' she bade her as her mother left the house. There was no answer, and Avena went to bed that night in the full knowledge that she was not flavour of the day with any of the Alladices, and that tomorrow she would be in for some cold-shoulder treatment from Tony and Martin. Which to her mind made it most odd that she found herself thinking of none of them when she finally lay down to sleep. The person she was thinking of was Nyall Lancaster; she had not known he was a bachelor.

He was far from her mind, however, the following morning when she bumped into Tony Spicer in the car park. 'Thanks very much for your support yesterday,' he snapped sarcastically.

'Good morning to you too. I'm feeling much better, thank you,' she retorted—well, she *might* have been unwell!

A week followed in which she was, as she had expected, well and truly cold-shouldered by the two directors. It did not worry her unduly; she had plenty of work to do that did not require too much consultation with them. If they wanted to be childish, let them get on with it, and, if it got too bad, she could always leave, she decided after a week of it.

However, the very next day, Friday, Tony came into her office, and from the warm 'Can I interrupt what you're doing, Avena?' with which he opened she knew that the cold war was over.

'Of course,' she smiled, feeling a tinge relieved; she preferred harmony to disharmony.

'The thing is, I've just had a phone call from Oakby Trading.'

'They're giving us an order!' she exclaimed, two steps ahead of him and feeling softened towards Nyall Lancaster because he had by no means slapped an embargo on Oakby's doing business with them.

'Not so fast.' Tony shook his head. 'Though we're much closer to being considered than we ever were.'

'Is that why they rang?' she queried, puzzled. To ring with such information seemed a mite odd.

'The thing is that following on from the Oakby headquarters opening they're having a trade evening this evening. This,' he went on quickly as her smell-a-rat antennae started to vibrate, 'will be a golden opportunity for us because it will be at a do such as tonight's that we might get a chance to talk business.'

'But . . . I thought trade evenings were designed to promote business for the host company, not the guest.'

'Well, that's true of course,' Tony blustered. 'But since they've been kind enough to extend an invitation to the three of us I'm not losing out on the smallest chance I get.'

'I'm included in this invitation?'

'You're an important member of our team.' He smiled. 'We couldn't function without you, Avena.' Soft soap! If she believed that she'd believe anything. 'Say you'll come,' he urged. 'It will be different this time,' he promised.

She guessed it would. This time, for certain, Nyall Lancaster would not be there. 'What time?' she asked, still wary, still not accepting.

'Any time between seven and eleven. We can go straight from here if you like—there's bound to be something to eat.'

On the face of it, it seemed innocent enough. But her suspicions still lingered. Tony's volte-face from frosty to smiling had been a bit sudden. True, it was the first time she'd seen him today, so he could have woken up thinking it was time to bury the hatchet.

She didn't like to be at odds with anyone either. She looked down at the cool, straight-skirted dress she had on, and reckoned it would pass muster.

'We won't have to stay the whole four hours?'

'Lord, no! Just show our collective face for an hour or so.'

'All right,' she agreed, and hostilities were over.

It was a warm evening. She sipped a long refreshing drink and chatted with people who came by and stopped for a chat. She was able to find an interest in most things people had to say, but at the same time she kept an eye open in case either Martin or Tony— who were in conversation on the other side of the hall from her—gave a sign that they might want her to join them.

For the moment, however, she was in conversation with an eager young man and his slightly older colleague. Perhaps soon she would be able to disappear to the ladies' room for a breather.

She did not get the chance, for just then someone addressed her from behind. The two men melted away and she turned around, and it was quite some minutes before she could make her escape.

She could not believe it. Nyall Lancaster! She was struck dumb. She had been certain, positive, he would not be there. Why would *he* put in an appearance at anything as unimportant as a trade evening? But he *was* there, standing right there in front of her, tall, dark, sophisticated and good-looking with it.

'I asked if you were now well again,' he repeated.

'Oh,' she gasped. 'I didn't expect to see you here.' Grief, how gauche that sounded! Avena made rapid strides to get herself back together again. 'Nor you to remember,' she added.

His cool look said that there was little that he ever forgot. 'Do you come to many of these affairs?' he enquired urbanely. He sounded surprised to see her there.

'I'm with Marton Exclusives,' she replied.

'I know.'

He would. If he remembered her from last week, and clearly he did, he would also remember the team she was with.

'You've met our two directors, Tony Spicer and Martin Usher.'

'But not you.'

'Well, that's remedied.' Somehow, while just talking to him made her insides shake, she held out her right hand. 'Avena Alladice,' she introduced herself.

'Call me Nyall,' he suggested, and she saw that he was aware from their conversation that he had no need to introduce himself.

She felt him take hold of her hand in a firm grip; her skin tingled. 'Do you come to many of these affairs?' she bounced his question back at him as he let go of her hand.

'Do you always wear your hair that way?'

'What's wrong with it?' she wanted to know, an instinctive hand going up to her golden chignon. She was not sure how she felt about personal questions.

'I didn't say anything was wrong with it. It suits you—but then I should imagine that with a face like yours, any style would suit you.' She had no answer to that, and he went on conversationally, 'As becoming as it is, I should like to see you with your hair out of that knot.'

The sauce of it! 'I think that's highly unlikely,' she replied coolly, and realised that he had cottoned on to the fact that she seldom wore her hair any way but the way it was now unless she was in bed when he smiled a silky kind of smile.

She was certain he was going to make some reference to it, and flicked him an aloof look for his trouble—only to be startled when he said nothing of the sort but challenged point-blank, 'You don't like me, do you?'

Her breath caught in her throat—this was bound to be good for business! Although, in all honesty, she did not know whether she liked him or not. She opened her mouth ready to protest that she didn't know him, found she was looking up into a pair of direct dark eyes, and heard herself ask, 'Are you going to hold it against me if I say no?'

Nyall Lancaster looked at her steadily for some moments, his dark gaze refusing to let her brilliant blue eyes look away. 'You mean hold it against Marton Exclusives?' he questioned, with no smile, no hint of anything. He was more astute than most, she realised, but she knew he had an honesty on a par with hers when he answered, 'No,' and then paused, before adding deliberately, 'Anything between you and me, Avena Alladice . . . is just between you . . . and me.'

Again, her breath caught—she didn't think she liked the sound of that. 'Forgive my bluntness, Mr Lancaster,' she drew every ounce of good manners to the fore to tell him, 'but there isn't anything between you and me. Er—or going to be,' she added for honest good measure.

God, what a man! That pointed 'Mr Lancaster' bounced straight off him. Not that she'd expected him to crumple anyway. But the steady look he favoured her with a moment before he bestowed on her the most devastating yet intimate smile threatened to make her legs buckle. 'Isn't there?' he murmured.

Heavens, he was serious! She knew it! Her heart pounded, her mouth went dry; never, she realised, had she met a man like him. He sounded all too clearly as if he meant business—but not the business she was hoping to gain.

It was difficult, not to say impossible, to get her head together while those relentless dark eyes stayed on her. But somehow she managed it. And it was with her usual forthrightness that she asked him straight out, 'What, exactly, do you want?'—and learned that, when it came to being forthright, Nyall Lancaster led the field.

For barely had her question left her lips when he replied, those dark eyes refusing to let her look away, 'You—in my bed.'

Her hand shook; she was glad she was halfway down the drink she held. She preferred plain speaking—but this was something else again. 'Some have tried,' she thought she should tell him.

'You're intimating that few have succeeded?' he enquired, a quizzical look coming to that half-smile he wore.

He wasn't going to let up; she sensed it, could almost feel it. She took a sip of her drink again, needing time to marshal her thoughts.

Now seemed the moment to put him right before this went any further. Plainly, he had seen her, and had thought to make another conquest. But, given that on top of everything else he had more charm than any one man had a right to have, she was not in line

to be a conquest of his, or any man's. Even while part
of her acknowledged that she could not deny she felt
attracted to him, even while part of her appreciated
his unflinching honesty, there were many more parts
of her that wanted more from a relationship than
just . . . bed.

She half turned from him to place her glass down
on a nearby table and, turning back, quietly reminded him, 'You implied that I could be honest with
you without it affecting the firm I work for.'

That hint of a smile had gone, and his look was
deadly serious as he reiterated, 'This is between you
and me, Avena. You can speak freely.'

Whatever else she did not know at that moment,
and she admitted that this man had an uncanny power
to disconcert her, what she did know, with a most
peculiar conviction since she barely knew him, was
that she could trust his word. That being so, she took
a deep breath, and felt slightly unnerved again when
he took his glance away from the blue of her eyes to
what one hopeful had once called her 'outstandingly
kissable' mouth.

Nyall Lancaster's gaze was back on her eyes,
however, when Avena determinedly began, 'Then I
have to tell you, Nyall——' She broke off, just his
first name on her lips undermining her. 'Er——' she
strove to get herself together again '—that I couldn't
go to bed with anyone I didn't love and—well—to be
honest, I'm not sure I even like you.'

There, it was said. He was intelligent; it showed in
his eyes. She was certain he must have read her
meaning—that there was just no chance that she
would ever go to bed with him.

She smiled; she felt she could afford to. He smiled; that smile worried her. 'Ah,' he said. But as she was wondering what that 'Ah' meant he engagingly added, 'An element of doubt.'

'What?'

'If you're unsure you like me that means there's a chance that you do.'

'Don't hold your breath!' she retorted. Really, he was the limit.

He laughed—there was no offending him, it seemed. Avena started to feel better. He was heady medicine, this man, but her little flare of anger seemed to have released the tension in her and, when all at once he took the conversation away from the designs he had on her and began to ask about her work, so, for the first time since meeting him, she began to relax.

'You're young to be finance director with Marton Exclusives,' he commented, adding before she could take exception to his remark, 'You must have worked very hard.'

She mentally thanked him for that, though thought it only right that she should tell him, 'Tony Spicer and Martin Usher are married to my two sisters.'

He did not show surprise at the news, so she guessed that he already knew about the family connection. But his comment surprised her instead. 'From what I've seen of Spicer, you wouldn't be head of finance if you weren't up to it.' Grief, how did he get to be so shrewd? 'Been doing the job long?' he enquired casually.

'I've been with Tony and Martin since I left school six years ago.'

'That makes you . . . ?'

She laughed; there was just something about this man. His look softened; he seemed to like the sound of her laugh and his eyes were on her mouth again. 'How old are *you*?' she was emboldened enough to ask.

'Thirty-five,' he replied without hesitation, but hinted, 'I did ask you first.'

'Twenty-two,' she felt honour-bound to reply.

'Ever been in love?' he tossed in.

'Never,' she answered, quite without thinking.

And she nearly dropped: his tossed-in question had clearly not been so throw-away or casual as she had thought.

'You're a virgin?' he queried, plainly referring to her statement that she could not go to bed with anyone she did not love.

Her mouth fell open, and only then did she realise that it had been a mistake to relax her guard. Yet, even while she could barely believe she was standing here having this conversation, she was replying, 'If you tell anyone I'll kill you.'

Amusement lit his face. Then he laughed, and she knew that whether or not he liked the sound of her laugh she definitely liked the sound of his. But, even while amusement was still dancing in his eyes, he drew himself to attention to request formally, 'May I, Miss Alladice, be the first?'

She wanted to laugh, but wouldn't. 'Get lost, Mr Lancaster,' she replied, and thought it was definitely high time that she headed for the ladies' room.

She walked away from him. 'May I be the first?' Indeed! No wonder Nyall Lancaster was at the top of his particular tree. All too clearly he was a man who knew what he wanted and went straight for it. He had come unstuck this time but, remembering how he had so easily disconcerted her, how her skin had tingled when they had shaken hands, she rather thought that she had done well to walk away from him unscathed. Without question, she acknowledged, Nyall Lancaster was dangerous!

Avena stayed as long as she could in the ladies' restroom, and realised that Nyall Lancaster must have had quite an effect on her when, just as she was about to leave, she found she had to take one very big deep breath.

She need not have worried, though, for when she returned to the large hall where the trade evening was taking place she could see not a sign of Nyall. Obviously he had stayed only a short while, and was now off on whatever was his usual Friday-night pursuit. Fleetingly it occurred to her that, if she had answered differently, she might now, at this very moment, be off to that 'whatever' with him. She blinked and was amazed at her thoughts. For heaven's sake, what was she thinking of? Then she saw that both Tony and Martin were heading her way.

'You seemed to be getting on very well with Nyall Lancaster,' Tony couldn't wait to remark.

Now didn't seem to be the time to tell Tony that her parting words to the man had been 'get lost'. 'He—er—was very interesting to talk to,' she murmured lightly.

'What did you talk about?' Martin wanted to know.

To tell them would result in their telling their wives, which also meant her mother, and she would hear about nothing for the next few months but Nyall Lancaster and how her incivility had lost the firm business.

'This and that,' she replied, sure in her mind that Nyall would not penalise Marton Exclusives because of her rejection of his request.

'What sort of "this and that"?' Tony insisted.

To say it was private would make him even more keen to know what had been said. 'We talked about finance—my job in finance,' she felt safe in revealing.

'You told him how solvent we were?' Tony pressed.

'I didn't have to,' she replied. 'It strikes me that Nyall Lancaster is a man who knows these things.' And before they could press further she added, 'Do you think it would matter if I went home now?'

Tony didn't. In fact, he seemed to think that she had done a good evening's work. She refused to feel guilty and went home to find her mother was out, so joined Mrs Parsons in the kitchen for half an hour, tucking into the *coq au vin* which the housekeeper had saved for her before going to her room to think about one Nyall Lancaster and to wish that she could get him out of her head.

Her mother, as usual, had her own plans for that weekend and on Saturday morning said that she would not miss her if she went down to her grandmother's and stayed overnight. 'You don't mind if I go?' Avena asked out of courtesy nevertheless.

'Not a bit,' Dinah Alladice replied. 'I'm golfing for most of today, and I promised Hugh I'd lunch with him tomorrow.' Hugh Edwards was an old friend of her mother.

'Enjoy,' Avena bade her, and drove down to Kembury, aware that Hugh wanted to marry her mother but that her mother already had her life the way she wanted it.

'Your room's ready, as it always is,' her grandmother greeted her when she arrived, and they spent
an enjoyable Saturday, her grandmother trotting off
to the village hall to play whist on Saturday evening—
and incidentally reminding Avena that she had
promised James Taylor that she would attend the
concert in her own village hall next Saturday. Avena
then fell to wondering about Nyall Lancaster—and
realised that her 'get lost' had severed, before it began,
a very physical relationship.

She was at work on Monday when she thought of
him again, and wished that she hadn't. She wanted
him out of her head in the same way that he was out
of her life—without ever having been in it apart from
a five-minute conversation—but he continually, and
when least expected, seemed to pop into her mind.

It was the same for the rest of the week too. She
would pick up some figure work with the intention
of really getting down to it and then discover that she
must have been staring into space for all of five
minutes with not a scrap of work done.

On Friday morning Avena decided that enough was
enough. It was highly unlikely that she would ever
bump into him again. He was, as she had repeated to
herself all that week, out of her life. She would put
all of her concentration into her work. Then the phone
rang.

She reached a hand to the instrument and picked
it up. 'Good morning, Avena,' Nyall said in her ear,
and she, who never blushed, went crimson.

Astonished at the effect this man had on her
emotions, she next heard a click as the switchboard
operator went off the line, and made hurried efforts
to recapture her composure. 'How are you, Nyall?'

she enquired, wondering why he was phoning but too open to pretend she hadn't recognised his cultured, all-masculine tones.

'Have dinner with me tomorrow?'

'Sweep me off my feet!' she laughed. No build-up, nothing. Truly a busy man, he thought of his objectives and, as she knew only too well, went straight for them.

'I've a meeting in five minutes.'

'Thank you for fitting me in.'

'Yes or no?'

Where was his charm of last Friday? 'Forgive me,' she replied, allowing a warm smile to creep into her voice, 'but I've a previous engagement.'

'Get out of it.'

The cheek of it! 'I don't want to! Besides, I promised James——' The line went dead. Avena threw her phone down on its rest. So I'm busy too! she fumed. Can you come out? No, I can't. Right, I'll go to my meeting. Who the devil did he think he was? What the devil did he think she was that, when she had seen nothing of him for a week, he thought all he had to do was to ring and she, panting to go out with him, would drop everything—and everyone—to do his bidding?

Suddenly, she laughed. She had to. Grief, she barely knew the man, and here she was getting all steamed up about him. Let him rot! She picked up her pen, relegated one Nyall Lancaster well and truly out of her life—then her office door opened and the two directors of the firm, who were straining every sinew to do business with one of his companies, came in.

'Well?' Tony questioned.

'Well what?'

'Don't be difficult, there's a dear,' Martin joined forces.

'Give me a clue?'

'What did he want?' Tony insisted, and added, as light began to dawn on her, 'I was passing Reception when I heard Gloria tell a Mr Lancaster ''just a moment'' and obviously I questioned her.'

'Obviously.'

Tony ignored her sarcasm. 'She said a Mr Nyall Lancaster had rung wanting to speak to you. So, since anything to do with him concerns us, what did he ring for?'

'You're not going to like it,' she answered pleasantly—Tony and his prying didn't deserve any better.

'He's told you he doesn't want us doing business with Oakby Trading?' Martin took a wild guess.

She shook her head. 'While it's quite apparent that Oakby Trading is of special interest to him—otherwise we wouldn't have seen him there on the two occasions we went—I'm sure he's got more confidence in his management there than to interfere and tell them who they shouldn't deal with.'

'Phew, that's a relief!' Martin exclaimed.

'So—why the call?' Tony was still intent on knowing.

'It was—um—personal.'

'Personal?'

Dammit—if she didn't tell him there was a fair chance that both Lucille and Coral would be at home when she got there that night. The two of them—in full harridan mode—plus her mother made a formidable trio. Anything for a quiet life. 'Nyall

Lancaster...asked me out,' she begrudgingly admitted.

'He *did*?' Both Tony and Martin looked as if they had some deal with Oakby Trading already signed and sealed.

'But I'm not going,' she told them bluntly before they could put their orders in for a yacht.

'Why not?' Tony demanded.

'I didn't realise it was in my contract!' she snapped, starting to get angry.

'Oh, come on, Avena, be fair. You know how important Oakby Trading would be to us.'

She did, and some of her anger faded. 'Yes, I know that. But that in no way makes it right for me to go out with anyone purely in some vague hope of doing business.'

'Hell's teeth!' Tony exclaimed. 'It's done all the time!'

'Not by me it isn't!'

'Oh, come on, love,' Martin coaxed. 'While I agree Nyall Lancaster is unlikely to interfere and tell the Oakby management team who they should *not* deal with, that's not to say they mightn't look favourably on any suggestion he might make about who they *should* deal with.'

'What did you say to him?' Tony wanted to know.

She was being pressured, and didn't like it. 'That I had a previous engagement.'

'Can't you cancel it?'

He was annoying her. 'I could—if I wanted to.'

'But you don't think sufficient of this firm, your sisters, and the disaster it would be for them not to have next season's fashions,' Tony inserted with cynical frankness, 'to do so.'

She'd leave. Damn the lot of them, she didn't have to put up with this; she'd leave.

'Would it cost you so much to break your date and give Nyall Lancaster a ring and tell him that you can make it tonight after all?' Tony persisted.

'Tomorrow night,' she corrected—but even as she did so a gem of a wonderful idea started to come to her. 'Nyall asked me out tomorrow, not tonight.'

Tony looked heartened by her use of Nyall's first name. 'Couldn't you see him—just to keep him—er—happy?' he wheedled.

He had no idea what he was asking. Avena didn't feel like telling him that the man he was urging her to go out with was more interested in bedding her than in taking her anywhere, and that thought made her angry too—with Nyall Lancaster. She thought of her promise to James Taylor that she would attend the concert in the village hall tomorrow evening. Strictly amateur. She thought of Nyall, sophisticated to the nth degree. She smiled. That should settle him!

She looked at Tony; it would get *him* off her back too. 'If you're sure I should do this,' she mumbled worriedly.

'Trust me!' Tony assured her with a smile.

'Very well,' she answered.

'We'll leave you to it,' he beamed, and ushered Martin out of her office.

Perhaps she should leave home as well as her job, she pondered. Life at home would be hell when Tony spread the word that she had taken the man he was trying to impress—the *sophisticated* man he was trying to impress—to a concert of local amateur talent in the village hall.

She stretched out a hand to the phone—and withdrew it. She suddenly felt nervous, on edge. She remembered that Nyall had been about to go to a meeting and left it for an hour. But an hour later she was again nervous and on edge, and was beginning to query the wisdom of what she was doing, when she picked up her phone and asked Gloria to get her Nyall Lancaster at Lancaster Holdings.

Her phone rang. She had been expecting it, but she jumped just the same. 'Mr Lancaster's not available,' Gloria relayed. 'But I've managed to get through to Philippa Drake, his PA. Will you speak to her?'

'Yes, please,' Avena agreed—and had to get on with it when the next second she heard a pleasant female voice on the line.

'I'm sorry Mr Lancaster isn't here to speak to you, Miss Alladice. Would you care to leave a message?'

As she had asked Gloria to get Nyall Lancaster Avena rather thought that Nyall must have asked Philippa Drake to get her, so his PA would have heard of her and know where she worked. But suddenly she experienced an aversion to Nyall's ringing her at her office.

'There's no message. I'll ring back,' she replied, and having obviated Gloria's being able to tell Tony, should he enquire, that Nyall Lancaster had rung again Avena rang off.

She would try again to contact Nyall, she knew. But, now that her anger had gone, she had started to worry. She did not immediately resume work but nibbled the end of her pencil. Somehow, she had a worrying feeling that, no matter how humble the venue, she was getting in a little over her head by asking Nyall Lancaster out anywhere.

CHAPTER THREE

IT HAD just gone four that afternoon when Avena put through her second call to Lancaster Holdings. 'It's Miss Drake again,' Gloria announced.

'I'll speak to her,' Avena said, and a moment later, 'Is Mr Lancaster available?' she was asking his PA.

'I'm afraid not, Miss Alladice,' Philippa Drake apologised, and Avena started to feel a shade discomfited and as if she was chasing him. Then she found that she had no need to feel in any way embarrassed when his PA quickly added, 'But I've been able to tell him you'd ring again, and Mr Lancaster asked me to give you his home number.'

Avena came off the phone wondering at this new experience for her. She was more used to men ringing her trying to fix up a date. This—that she seemed to be chasing Nyall Lancaster for one—was a first. She did not like it. Even if it was only in response to his asking her out that she was trying to contact him, she did not like it.

Nor would she be trying to contact him at all were it not for the fact that the directors 'Grimm' needed a touch of come-uppance—she couldn't wait to see their faces on Monday when she told them that she had taken the man they held in such high esteem to an amateur concert in the village hall. Come to think of it, she couldn't wait to see Nyall's face either. The sauce of it—thinking she would fall into bed with him!

She drove home in a happier frame of mind, but, while she was not the panicky sort, she owned that she felt quite panicky when she realised that she had better ring Nyall straight away. If he was going out for the evening, she could well miss him.

She dialled his number from her room, and as the number started to ring out so nerves started to bite, and she could not think of one single solitary line that would give her an introduction to what she wanted to say.

Then the phone was answered. 'Lancaster!'

'Er—hello,' she managed, suddenly realising that her throat had gone quite dry. 'Avena Alladice,' she added as her power to think of anything else to say deserted her.

There was a pause. Then, referring to the fact that this was the third phone call she'd made in her endeavours to speak to him, 'You're keen,' he drawled.

And Avena's panic evaporated. 'I love you too!' she retorted, and decided that she didn't want to go out with him after all. The fact that she had phoned him to try would have to satisfy Tony and Martin. But, silently, Nyall was waiting for her to say why she *had* been trying to get him. 'You don't—um—really want to see me tomorrow, do you?' she asked.

And she didn't know quite how she felt when, in his usual forthright manner, he replied, 'I wouldn't have wasted my time phoning you this morning if I didn't.'

'I'm not going to sleep with you!' She laid it on the line before he could draw another breath.

'Who said anything about sleep?' he tossed at her before she could blink, and she just had to laugh—he was the end.

There was a pause, and she guessed that the light sound of her laughter must have reached him when, a hint of good humour there in his voice, 'I suppose you know you're gorgeous,' he commented.

'I believe somebody did mention it once,' she smiled, realising that she wanted to laugh again. Honestly, this man! She fought hard to get her head together. 'Actually,' she began, 'the reason I rang...the—er—reason I've been trying to contact you...'

'You're desperate to see me after all?' he stepped in to help her out.

'I'm feeling desperate—to some degree,' she owned, but was not sure then whether that desperation came from her sudden seeming inability to ask him out— as if she feared the outcome in some way, which was ridiculous—or whether it came from the coercion which Tony and Martin were trying to use. All at once, she realised she was feeling very much confused.

'You're being pressured?' Nyall asked quietly, perceptively, all sign of good humour gone from his voice.

She remembered Tony's 'you don't think sufficient of this firm, your sisters...' and rather thought she was. 'Yes,' she admitted, knowing from his promise that she could speak freely and trust him that it would not affect the firm.

'I'm not sure that I care very much for that,' he said, and she warmed to him because, while the fact that he wanted her in his bed still stood, he seemed to care not at all for having someone else pressure her into being friendly towards him.

'Do you know, Nyall, I could quite get to like you?'

'I trust you'll allow me to work on that,' he returned, his good humour back. And she wanted to laugh again and stopped wondering why she should feel confused from time to time when she was talking to him.

Time to get down to the purpose of her call, though all at once it dawned on her that, with all that Nyall had got going for him, there was every chance that by now he'd got someone else lined up for tomorrow night. Rarely, she guessed, if ever, would anyone turn him down.

'The thing is, Nyall—um——' Stop messing about, she told herself. There was only one way to say this. 'Are you still free tomorrow night?' she plunged.

'Your date has let you down?'

'Would he?' she scoffed, and laughed because he did. Then she added, 'Nor would I use you as second-best.'

'Flatter me!' he retorted drily.

Her mouth curved upwards. 'My previous engagement still stands, but...'

'I'm listening.'

'Um—well...' Suddenly she blew it. 'It's nothing sophisticated, or anything like that,' she said, when she hadn't meant to say anything of the sort. Confused? The man made a nonsense of her. 'But—you could come with me if you like.'

His answer was wary but decisive. 'I've a feeling I'm going to regret this—but count me in.'

'You don't know what it is yet!'

'So?'

Laughter bubbled up inside her. 'Are you always this—um—bold?'

'What time?'

Avena judged that he hadn't got where he was by being timid. 'Could you get here by six-thirty?' she asked. 'Oh, you don't know my address. It's——'

'I know it,' Nyall cut in, and put down his phone.

Quite clearly, he must have a date for that evening and considered that he had spent enough time getting his recreation for the following evening fixed up. Any small annoyance she felt about that, though, was negated by the realisation that he must be truly interested in her, or why would he have bothered to find out her address?

Interested! Good Lord, what was she thinking of? Any man who stated, as he had, that he wanted her in his bed had to be *interested*. But why she should feel annoyed that he couldn't wait to finish their conversation because he had other fish to fry was beyond her. Confusion wasn't in it! She later went to bed hoping that tomorrow night's concert would bore the socks off him.

Her sisters were at her home almost before she had finished her breakfast the next morning. 'Mother isn't down yet,' she told them as they joined her at the breakfast-table—she knew as well as they did that, this morning, it was not their mother that the dynamic duo were there to see.

'Oh, isn't she?' Coral questioned innocently.

'We'll just have a cup of coffee while we're waiting,' Lucille added.

They looked at her meaningfully, and the fact that they seemed to think she would go and collect a couple of cups and saucers did nothing to improve her opinion that they were a lazy pair. Other days she might have gone on their unspoken bidding. Today, knowing full well that she would shortly be on the receiving end of their indelicate probing, unwanted advice, and possibly—according to how it went—some verbal unpleasantness, she didn't feel like it.

'You know where the kitchen is,' she hinted.

'Well, of course,' Coral replied. 'But this isn't our home any longer.' Wasn't it? From what Avena saw and heard, her two elder sisters spent more time in their old home than they ever did in their own. 'I just thought...'

'Be my guest,' Avena smiled, and again fleetingly thought of moving out.

She wondered how long it would take them to get round to the reason for their early visit—only long enough for Coral to come back from the kitchen with the china and a fresh pot of coffee—no doubt made by Mrs Parsons—was the answer.

'By the way, Tony mentioned that you were dating Nyall Lancaster,' Lucille murmured as if giving her full concentration to the sweetener she was dropping into her coffee.

Dating? One date was dating? 'Oh, yes?' Avena queried—her sister would put the KGB to shame—but she wasn't biting.

'That was quick work!' Coral opined.

'I've known him for over a week,' Avena replied, when she hadn't meant to give out any information.

'Is this your first date with him?' Lucille wanted to know.

All too evidently they had both been filled in, chapter and verse, by their husbands.

'Yes,' and hoping to end it right there, 'and it'll probably be the last.'

'Oh, for heaven's sake, Avena!' And they were off. His wealth, his standing, his life. Her life, their lives, the business—and how the universe hung on her having a second date with Nyall Lancaster.

It was time, Avena thought, to take herself off. She stood up, cutting Lucille off in full flow. 'Oh, if you see Mother before you go——' they'd be galloping up those stairs as soon as she had the outer door shut '—you might mention to her that I'm going out this evening.' As if they wouldn't!

Avena escaped, sickened by the pair of them. She loved them, but really most times they, with their greedy, avaricious ways, were the living end!

It was a superb summer's day. Avena went into town and purchased a few toiletries and a pair of sandals and returned home to find that her sisters had gone and her mother was on the point of going out to join some friends for lunch.

'Where are you going tonight, dear?' her mother enquired as a by-the-way as she walked towards the front door.

'I'm going to a concert with a friend,' seemed to be the best answer—her parent would have apoplexy if she knew which concert she was taking Nyall to. 'Are you out this evening?' she asked as a countermeasure. Rarely did her mother stay in on a Saturday evening.

'I'm having dinner with Hugh. He's calling for me at seven. What time are you going out?'

'Half-past sixish,' Avena replied.

'Is Mr Lancaster calling for——?' Her mother broke off, realising she had slipped up—Avena had said only that she was going to a concert with a friend.

She smiled sympathetically; her mother was usually more careful than that. 'I'll introduce you if you're down,' Avena offered—and straight away wished she hadn't, because now there was no chance that she would be able to just slip out when she saw Nyall's car coming up the drive.

She went into the kitchen and had a cup of coffee with Mrs Parsons when her mother had gone, and discovered that her mother had forgotten to tell the housekeeper that she would be eating out that evening when Mrs Parsons asked her if she thought it would be all right to leave a casserole for her mother to warm through. Another five-minute conversation brought forth the information that Mrs Parsons was baby-sitting for her adored grandson that evening. Another five minutes and Avena, having learned that their housekeeper had been asked to stay overnight, was giving her the weekend off.

'Oh, but I couldn't!' Mrs Parsons protested.

Half an hour later Avena was waving her off down the drive. Mrs Parsons had taken some persuading but she had been able to convince her that should her mother want tea that afternoon, then she would make it for her. In the unlikely event that her mother would want breakfast in the morning she would make that too and, if her mother had not arranged to have lunch out tomorrow as she usually did, she would take her out somewhere.

There was plenty to eat in the house, Avena saw when she returned to the kitchen: various meats and cheeses. She made herself an egg salad, and went up to her room to check on her wardrobe.

She later heard her mother come in and went to tell her that she had given Mrs Parsons the rest of the weekend off. 'She works hard and if we're to keep her it won't hurt to——'

'You don't need to go on,' Dinah Alladice interrupted her, and, in agreement, it seemed, smiled at her youngest.

'Would you like some tea?' Avena offered.

'Oh, I couldn't eat or drink another thing. Thank goodness there are a good few hours to go before Hugh calls and I have to eat again.'

Avena smiled; her mother had a hard life. 'I think I'll go and wash my hair,' she remarked, and wished she hadn't when her mother looked speculatively at her—every bit as if she thought she was making a special effort for Nyall Lancaster!

Grief, Avena thought, slightly cross as she stood under the shower and got to work with the shampoo, she was always washing her hair! There was nothing special about her date with Nyall. Well, maybe there was, she qualified, in that after sitting through this evening's performance he would never ask her out again. And she didn't give a button about that.

The nearer it got to six-thirty, however, the more she began to feel a kind of anxiety in her stomach. Anxiety! Perhaps not anxiety. Excitement, then. Oh, grief, she must be cracking up, she scoffed, and, fifteen minutes to go before Nyall arrived, found she had gone to glance out of her bedroom window as if looking for him.

She heard her mother leave her bedroom and go upstairs, and realised that it was a foregone conclusion that her mother would be ready and waiting to see Nyall when he drove up. What she had not realised, though, nor expected, was that both her sisters would be there too!

Scarcely able to believe her eyes, she recognised Lucille's car as it turned into the drive. Coral was in the passenger seat, so Lucille must have picked her up on the way. They had come solely to meet Nyall to see what he was like—she knew it!

Shame and mortification stormed through her as she came away from the window. How dare they? she fumed, and, two minutes later, rushed from her room to give her sisters a piece of her mind and attempt to get them to leave before he arrived.

They still had keys to their old home and were letting themselves in as she reached the hall. 'What the . . . ?' was as far as she got before her mother came out into the hall from the drawing-room, took one look at her, and plainly did not think much of the way she was dressed to go out with such an influential man.

'Good gracious, Avena!' she exclaimed. 'You can't go out looking like *that.*'

Avena spun round. 'What's the matter with the way I look?' she asked—and had two elder sisters tearing in to tell her.

'You can't go to a concert dressed like that!' Lucille exclaimed.

'What in creation have you done to your hair?' Coral asked, not taken with the single plait down the centre of Avena's back.

'You're not wearing tights!' her mother exclaimed, horrified.

'It's hot, and besides . . .' Avena found herself on the defensive.

'Can anybody join in?' asked a cool, amused, all-masculine voice from the open doorway—and Avena nearly died from the embarrassment of it.

'Nyall—hello—come in,' was the stilted best she could manage as she hoped against hope that, having just come in from brilliant sunshine, he might miss in the shady hall the fact that she had gone a furious red. 'I'll—er—just go up and get my bag,' she added, and turned swiftly about, only to have to turn back again when her mother reminded her of her manners.

'Aren't you going to make any introductions, dear?' she asked sweetly.

'I'm sorry,' Avena apologised, and strove hard to gain her composure, on which she seemed to have a very fragile hold when Nyall was around but which now, in her embarrassment, seemed to have deserted her completely. Swiftly she made the introductions, but couldn't look Nyall in the eye. And once everyone had shaken hands she murmured a swift, 'Excuse me,' and, trying not to run, went quickly up the stairs.

'Come into the drawing-room, Nyall,' she heard her mother invite, and could have burst into tears.

She rapidly went off the idea of taking Nyall to the concert. Her notion of perhaps thumbing her nose at him and her brothers-in-law didn't seem nearly as clever now as it had done before. She didn't want to go. No way did she want to go down those stairs again either. But she had promised James Taylor and, oh, heavens, she had no idea what her mother and sisters were saying, asking, subtly prying—but not subtly enough for Nyall not to see through—at this very moment.

Suddenly she was galvanised into action; she grabbed up her bag, and went quickly down the stairs and into the drawing-room. 'Ready?' Nyall enquired, and was on his feet bidding pleasant adieus to the three women who had been entertaining him in her absence. He said nothing more until they had closed the front door. 'Like the hair,' he commented.

'I said it was nothing sophisticated,' she reminded him stiffly; her loose cotton frock and sandals had seemed just right earlier.

They went to his car. He had locked it automatically but now unlocked it, took off his jacket, transferred his wallet to his trousers, and took off his tie, throwing them on to the back seat. 'Unsophisticated enough?' he asked, coming round to where she stood and showing himself for her approval.

Had she not been feeling so uptight she would have been amused. But she could not so much as raise a smile. He looked at her levelly for a moment or two, then silently leaned down and opened the passenger door for her.

'Can we walk?' she blurted out. Her nerves were all on edge; she didn't want to sit in his car—she needed to walk. 'It's only ten minutes away.'

'Nice evening for it,' he commented, and locked up his car. Then they started down the drive.

'You needn't come!' she said abruptly when they reached the bottom of the drive.

'What—after I've taken such pains with my appearance?' he teased, and suddenly she began to feel a whole lot better. 'You'll have to watch that—you almost smiled then,' he remarked, and she realised that he must have been watching her.

'I'm sorry,' she apologised, adding, although it was in no way an explanation, 'Lucille and Coral—they arrived a minute before you did.'

'But you weren't expecting them,' he observed astutely.

'I'd seen them this morning.'

'They were over at first light?'

'How did...?' Her voice faded.

'I hope we can always be honest with each other, Avena,' Nyall said quietly, and she stopped, and as he stopped she looked up at him.

'Even if someone else is involved?'

'You already have my assurance on that.'

'You won't hold it against Tony and Martin that it was because of them that I rang you?'

'And there was I thinking it was my fatal charm,' he sighed.

Her lips twitched, and they fell into step again. 'Tony heard our switchboard operator taking your call...'

'Which is why you left a message for me not to ring you back.'

'You're sharper than a laser!' she exclaimed, but admitted, 'Tony and Martin came to see me and must have told my sisters when they got home that I'd be ringing you.'

'Then look on the bright side,' Nyall suggested.

'Bright side?'

'Your sisters could have rushed over to see you last night.'

She laughed. 'Can I apologise again for letting it get to me?'

'You don't have to,' Nyall said understandingly. 'You were embarrassed because you're warm and sensitive. And,' he added, 'I like that about you.'

There it was, his charm again; Avena knew she was growing to like him—and thought him more dangerous than ever. 'We're here,' she told him as they approached the village hall. She dared a look at him, saw that he was taking in the village hall entrance where a few eight-year-olds darted in and out of a few eighty-year-olds.

'I believe I overheard one of your sisters referring to a concert,' he recalled, but looked completely unfazed as he muttered, 'You're too good to me, Miss Alladice.'

The concert was due to start at seven prompt, and Avena realised as she and Nyall took their places in a row of plastic seats that from being so uptight that she had been perilously close to tears she was suddenly feeling very much better.

At five past seven the concert began, and Avena couldn't resist a small peek at Nyall as a seven-year-old scraped her way through a violin solo. His face was straight—that was a blessing. She could not have forgiven him had he been laughing. He even joined in the thunderous, mostly familial, applause afterwards. Act followed act: a singer, a pianist, a recitation, and another singer. Then it was the interval.

'Would you like a cup of tea?' she asked.

'Love one,' he accepted solemnly.

He was buying raffle tickets from James Taylor when she got back with two teas. 'I didn't think you'd come!' James exclaimed, tearing off a couple of strips and handing them to Nyall.

'I said I would. If I remember rightly, I promised,' she smiled.

James beamed. 'That was weeks ago. I didn't think you'd remember.'

'Shall I have some raffle tickets, James?' she asked. It was all in a good cause.

'Your boyfriend got you some,' James answered. 'I'm on first next half,' he informed them chirpily, and worked his way to the next row.

'See where coming to a concert in the village hall will get you,' she murmured to Nyall. He could not have missed hearing James refer to him as her boyfriend.

'I'm hoping to be more than that,' he returned softly in her ear, and Avena knew she was right to think him dangerous. Nyall didn't want to be anything as cosy as her boyfriend—he wanted to be her lover. He had said so.

The audience had warmed up by the second half and although James fluffed a note here and there he performed his accordion solo very well. Other acts followed and, when she could not resist taking another glance at Nyall, Avena saw that he actually seemed to be quite at home and enjoying it!

Feeling slightly stunned, she forgot all about the fact that this was meant to punish him for his nerve, and, at this evidence of a man who she knew must have wined and dined and attended first-class performances at top-notch theatres, could not help but warm to him.

So much so, in fact, that when the concert was over and they had stopped to chat here and there for a few minutes before walking back to her home she found herself asking, 'Would you like to come in for supper?'

Nyall consulted his watch. 'It's half-past nine,' he stated, and although she was certain that there were some nights when he didn't make it back home at all he astonished her by saying, 'It's a bit late for me, I'm afraid.' But he added, in the face of her disbelieving look, 'However, in your case, I'll make an exception.'

Her lips twitched. 'Our housekeeper has the weekend off,' she told him as she led the way to the kitchen.

He drew a chair out from the table and sat down and, clearly not intending to assist, asked, 'Can I do anything to help?'

'You can't have had anything to eat for ages,' she suddenly realised as she washed her hands at the kitchen sink.

'The things I do for you, Avena Alladice.'

'How do you like your steak?' she enquired, going to the fridge.

'As it comes,' he risked it.

'You're a model guest.'

'Do you have many?'

'I don't bring many men home, if that's what you're asking,' she replied, checking the grill and hunting up some spaghetti and olive oil.

'How about concerts? Do you take many a walk to the village hall?'

'Didn't I tell you? You're favoured,' she grinned, and really liked him when he didn't try to make capital out of that remark but grinned back, and then sat silently watching her as she took a wedge of Roquefort cheese and began slicing it up.

Inside half an hour they were both seated at the kitchen table tucking into steak with grilled Roquefort on top, and spaghetti which had been boiled and drained and mixed in with the bits of cheese and meat juices left behind in the grill-pan.

Avena became aware of him watching her and looked up from her meal and across the table at him. His eyes were on her face. 'Have I a smut on my nose?' she asked.

'Even a smut on your nose wouldn't detract from your beauty,' he replied seriously, and she suddenly knew that he meant it.

Her heart fluttered unexpectedly, and she was confused again and needed, quite desperately needed, to say something, anything, to get her over the next few moments. 'Er—see what being born on a Monday does for a girl,' she said lightly, and hoped that he would think any small heat in her otherwise delicate colouring came from her close proximity to the grill earlier.

'You're a Monday's child?'

She nodded. 'Is your steak all right?' she asked, in an attempt to get his attention away from her.

'Perfect,' he replied, but was not so easily sidetracked, she discovered. 'Monday's child is . . . ?' She didn't answer and could see that he was digging into the deeper recesses of his mind. 'Monday's child is fair of face,' he brought out of a dark nowhere, and for long moments looked into the beautiful blue of her eyes and at the fairness of her face.

Speechlessly Avena looked back at him and her heart pounded again, and she just didn't know what it was about him that he could do that to her. 'My grandmother's seventy-two and has just booked to go on a cruise,' she blurted out apropos of nothing.

He didn't actually say, Take a sledge-hammer to change the subject, but it was there in his look. 'That's nice,' he drawled. But, taking pity on her—she might not have been blushing but she felt ridiculous inside— he asked conversationally, 'Does your grandmother live with you?'

'She has a cottage in Worcestershire.'

'You're close to her,' he all at once realised. It was a statement, not a question.

'How did you know that?'

He shrugged. 'Matter of simple deduction,' he replied. 'While your mother and sisters have beauty too, you are not the same.'

'I'm not?' She knew that she was a vastly different person from her mother and her sisters, but how, in the short while Nyall had been alone with them while she had been upstairs collecting her bag, had he so swiftly been able to discern it too?

'You stand apart,' he commented briefly, and, finishing up the last of his steak and spaghetti, stated, 'That was splendid.' He looked levelly at her to enquire, 'Is your life always this good, Avena?'

'This simple, you mean?' she asked, unoffended, and thought about it for a second or two. Having recently thought a couple of times about leaving her job, her home, 'It will do for the moment,' she answered lightly.

'No plans to marry?' he wanted to know.

She looked at him and smiled. 'Not for money, so don't get worried.'

She saw his lips twitch. 'You wouldn't marry for money?'

Avena thought of her sisters. In spite of a hiccup or two when money had been comparatively tight, there was little they wanted for these days—but look at them; neither Lucille nor Coral was happy. 'I want to be happy,' Avena stated, and added a little defiantly, she had to own, 'And if you think that's corny I don't care.'

Again she was pinned by his dark look. 'I hope you get what you want,' he commented. Then suddenly he smiled, and there was a wicked gleam in his eyes. 'And me,' he added. Avena stared at him, knowing without doubt what he was referring to.

'I . . .' she gasped, and was totally confused again.

Suddenly the atmosphere between them became electric. He stood up. 'I was going to offer to do the washing-up but—perhaps you'd better show me out,' he suggested.

She had been going to poke around in the freezer for ice-cream, or at least offer him coffee. But she was feeling tense all at once and decided that perhaps he was right and maybe it *was* time for him to go. She also got to her feet.

She walked outside with him to his car and, once they were away from the close confines of the house, her tension eased and the atmosphere became far less charged. She could only guess that Nyall had recognised that when, car keys in hand, he did not immediately get into his car and go but lingered a minute or so longer.

'Thank you for taking me to the concert,' he trotted out like some well-brought-up schoolboy, and Avena could hear the smile in his voice.

'My pleasure,' she began to trot back, when her innate honesty came along and tripped her up. 'Er— I'm sorry, Nyall, but I have to confess—you weren't— er—supposed to enjoy it.'

In the light from the porch lamp he studied her slightly ashamed expression, but to her amazement, remarked easily, 'Oh, I know that, Avena Alladice, I know that.'

'You do, and you came just the same?' She couldn't believe it.

'You're not the first beautiful woman to ring up and ask me out, it's true, but you're the only one I've ever accepted.'

'Because?' She was intrigued to know.

He leant an arm casually on his car. 'Well, to begin with, I asked you out, so I knew that you were more chased than chasing. Add to that the spirit you'd shown in not hanging around to be introduced at my bidding.'

'I'm sorry about that,' she apologised, though she had never thought she would. 'Tony said I'd got to be nice to you, and...' She faltered, thinking of her sisters, and while family loyalty kept her silent on that score she had to own, 'It—er—goes against the grain to be—um——'

'Nice to men for what you can get out of them?' Nyall finished for her, seeming—astonishingly, to her mind—to know her far, far better than her brothers-in-law did. She was not sure how she felt about him knowing her so well, but he was going on. 'When you phoned last night—you, Avena the Proud, ringing me for the third time—I knew to be wary.'

'You're much too smart.'

'I know. When it became apparent that you, Avena the Spirited, were under pressure to ring me, I just knew that you had something dastardly up your sleeve.'

Guilt smote her and she looked down at her feet. Then the spirit he had seen in her gave her a nudge and she looked swiftly up. 'But you enjoyed the concert,' she grinned.

'I got to meet James.'

'James! Did I mention him before...?'

'You said you'd a previous engagement which you didn't want to get out of. That you'd promised James... I thought you meant that he was your date for this evening.'

She stared at him, startled again. 'But you never referred to James when I rang and asked you to come...'

'His loss was my gain,' Nyall shrugged. 'Tough luck on him.'

Her eyes went wide. 'Are you always so—so ruthless?' she asked.

'Always,' he confirmed. But added when she just stood and silently stared at him, 'Though I can be quite cute sometimes.'

What could she do? She laughed. And Nyall grinned. Then, standing away from his car, he stretched out his hands to her shoulders and, holding her, bent down and gently kissed her lightly parted lips.

'You're pretty cute yourself, come to think of it,' he murmured, and, while she was standing there speechless, he got into his car and drove off.

Avena stood exactly where she was for several minutes after he had gone, her fingers on the lips which he had so gently kissed. What was it about the man that since she had known him she had also known more confusion than she could ever remember? Because of her embarrassment that her sisters had driven over especially to inspect him she had come closer to tears than she had in years—and yet Nyall could make her want to laugh like no other man could!

And never had she expected the evening to turn out as well as it had. She had—enjoyed it! Actually enjoyed it!

She was still shaken about that as she slowly went into the house and closed the door.

CHAPTER FOUR

IT WAS Sunday—nothing to rush around for—but Avena was awake early and got out of bed to go and stare out of her bedroom window. For once, however, she did not see the pleasantness of her surroundings but looked out and remembered the previous evening.

Truth to tell, it had been a splendid evening. Though in being truthful she felt slightly stunned to realise that she had enjoyed having supper with Nyall as much as the concert. Had enjoyed his company... And what about him? He had seemed to enjoy the evening too.

She pondered a great deal about him. Bed was definitely his aim; he hadn't balked from saying so. Yet, last night, he had kissed her gently and had gone... All at once Avena saw that he was far, far more subtle than she had realised and she knew then that, should he ring her again, she would have to watch her step. Not that she was likely to give in to him anyway. Good grief, oranges would turn to lemons first.

Avena left the window and went and showered and dressed. She had attended to the washing-up last night but she'd better go and tidy round so that everything was as Mrs Parsons would like it when she returned.

'How did you get on last night?' her mother enquired when she surfaced later that morning.

'Had a good evening,' Avena answered honestly, and, perhaps hoping to avoid any more questions, added, 'Would you like some breakfast?'

'Just coffee,' her mother replied. But before Avena could escape to the kitchen she asked, 'Where did you go?'

Oh, dear. 'There was a concert in the village hall. We——'

'You never took a man of Mr Lancaster's position to a village concert?' her mother exclaimed in alarm.

'He enjoyed it,' Avena declared, and made for the door, but her mother hadn't finished yet.

'Where did you go afterwards?' she wanted to know, apparently fully aware that village hall concerts were in the habit of finishing early.

'We—er—had supper.'

'Where? That new place Lucille was telling——?'

'Here actually,' Avena cut in, knowing that there was going to be the devil to pay but wanting it all over quickly.

'Here? But...you'd given Mrs Parsons the weekend off! You——'

'I cooked us something. We ate in the kitchen and——'

'You ate in the *kitchen*!' Dinah Alladice gasped in astonishment. 'You're telling me that you didn't know better than to entertain Mr Lancaster *in the kitchen*!' she echoed in shocked tones.

'He—er—enjoyed it,' Avena repeated, but as her mother recovered was obliged, out of courtesy, to suffer a lecture on the rights and wrongs of the matter: what she should and should not do in future and—for some obscure reason her grandmother was dragged into it—her mother's view that her grandparent was a bad influence.

At last Avena escaped to the kitchen, knowing quite well that her grandmother would say 'Good' should she repeat her mother's view of her influence on her.

It was a sobering thought, though, that since her mother was bound to be on the hot line to her sisters within the next hour—if her sisters weren't on the phone to their parent before then—then via them Tony and Martin would soon know everything. To leave her home and her job again seemed to be a very good idea.

Avena came closer than ever to handing in her resignation the next morning when, before she had started her day, Tony Spicer came into her office.

'For God's sake, Avena, what the devil do you think you're playing at?' he asked, thoroughly disgruntled; she knew full well what he was talking about.

'It was you who asked me to ring Nyall and——'

'I didn't ask you to take him to the local amateur night!'

'My mistake—you didn't stipulate where we should go!'

'Dammit, Avena, use your head. You know we're trying to do business——'

'Not through me, you're not!' she retorted, rattled, and was on the point of saying that she was leaving when he cut in.

'You've made damned sure of that, haven't you? It's highly unlikely Nyall Lancaster will phone you a second time.'

'Terrific!' Avena replied crisply, and there followed a heated, unpleasant argument which ended a few minutes later with Tony slamming out of her office.

It was terrific, too, she fumed. Tony was now under no doubt whatsoever that she could not be used to further the business. It was now categorically most firmly established that he and Martin would be wasting their time in trying to get her anywhere near Oakby Trading ever again. And it was assured that there would be no further pressure from any of them, her sisters included.

And, having cleared the air on that score, Avena realised as the day wore on that she was beginning to feel a good deal better—so much so that when Fergus Bradley phoned she agreed to meet him for a drink that evening, even though she knew in advance that almost the entire time would be spent in dissecting where he had gone wrong in relation to his ex-wife, her friend Kate.

As anticipated the evening went by on leaden feet; Fergus wasn't any nearer to getting over Kate, Avena discovered. 'Thanks for listening,' he said on parting.

'What are friends for?' she replied gently, and hurried home to ask her mother casually if there had been any phone calls for her while she had been out.

'None. Who were you expecting to ring?' her mother enquired, her tone a degree or two on the chilly side, so obviously either Lucille or Coral had been in touch to keep her up to date with the latest printout of Avena's misdeeds. Her mother's voice sharpened. 'You surely weren't expecting Mr Lancaster to phone?'

'Grief, no!' Avena denied, and took herself off to bed feeling a shade out of sorts. Nyall wouldn't ring her at the office again, she knew that. But... well, he might, despite Tony's 'It's highly unlikely', have phoned her at home.

Nyall did not phone on Tuesday evening either, and Avena was certain she didn't care a jot anyway. The phone stayed dead on Wednesday and Thursday evening too, and on Friday Avena decided that she would go down to her grandmother's that evening and spend the weekend there.

Saturday was a beautiful sunny day but even as she helped her grandmother in the garden her thoughts kept straying to Nyall and how her thought of should he ring her again of Sunday had now become a positive he would never ring again.

She and her grandmother were having a cup of tea on the lawn that afternoon when Avena decided that no matter what her mother, her sisters, her brothers-in-law or anyone else thought she just could not believe, from the admittedly little she knew of Nyall, that he would be put off by attending a local concert and afterwards eating supper in the kitchen. It just did not seem to go with the man she had, well, seemed so compatible with that evening. Which left her with no other course but to realise that Nyall had gone off her.

'You're still worried, Avena?'

'Sorry?' Avena came away from her thoughts to realise that her grandmother must have been watching her.

'You didn't look too happy just then.'

'I'm fine, darling,' Avena replied lightly. Strangely, although she had always been able to confide in her grandmother about everything, she somehow felt unable just then to confide in her about Nyall. Nor, for that matter, could she tell her about her mother blowing a fuse because of her entertaining Nyall in the kitchen.

'Are you still off Tony and Martin?' her grandmother probed lightly.

'I've been giving more thought to your suggestion that I leave,' Avena confessed.

'My suggestion was that you tell them you're leaving, not that you actually leave,' her grandmother reminded her. 'Though you'd have no trouble getting another job anywhere. Any half-decent employer would snap you up.'

'Oh, Gran,' Avena laughed. 'You and your rose-coloured glasses.' Her grandmother smiled her fond smile, and from there Avena changed the subject to ask how her holiday plans were going.

'Did I tell you that I'll be flying to join the cruise ship?' she replied. 'Ask your mother if I can stay overnight. It won't be as tiring if I drive to the airport from your place than if I drive straight from here.'

'Of course you can stay,' Avena said promptly. 'You can leave your car with us and I'll drive you to the airport.'

'What do you think I am, old or something?'

'You're lovely,' Avena laughed. And the next day she drove home in a happier frame of mind than she had been.

Not that she'd been unhappy, she determinedly decided. Nyall Lancaster could stuff his phone calls. Grief, she'd never waited a phone call from a man in her life; she wasn't about to start now!

She let herself into the house to hear the sound of the telephone ringing. There was no sign of her mother being at home, and Mrs Parsons might be out; Avena raced to answer it.

She picked it up, barely realising that she had been panicked by the thought that it might have stopped ringing before she got to it, and gasped, 'Hello?'

'You're out of breath!' grated a voice she would know anywhere.

Huh! He thought he could leave it a week between phone calls and she'd be pleased to hear from him. 'Who wouldn't be breathless to hear you on the phone?' she lobbed back at him.

'Bloody woman!' he snarled.

Cheeky pig! She wanted to laugh. 'What do *you* want?' she snapped aggressively.

'Where have you been?' he demanded.

'That's absolutely none of your business!' she retorted before curiosity got the better of her. 'How do you know I've been anywhere?'

'I rang on Saturday. You weren't there.'

'So I've been away for the weekend.' Her curiosity overcame her again. 'Why did you ring?'

'I happened to have a couple of theatre tickets.'

And he thought that, at the last minute, he could ring her and she'd rush to go out with him! 'I trust you were able to find somebody else to take?' she fired crossly.

'Naturally,' he drawled, but again demanded, 'So where did you go this weekend?'

She'd be damned if she'd tell him. 'It's got nothing to do with you where I've been—or who with,' she added, realising that she didn't care much for his 'naturally' a moment ago—as if he'd got women queuing up waiting for his phone calls.

'You've been away with someone?' he barked hostilely.

Damn him to hell! Who did he think he was that he could bark his questions at her and expect an answer? 'Let's put it this way—you don't even stand a chance of being second.'

His phone crashed down in her ear but she did not regret a word of what she had just said. So what if, by alluding to his 'may I be first?', her 'you don't even stand a chance of being second' had as good as told him that she had lost her virginity that weekend. He'd had all week to ring her and ask her to the theatre. Not that she would have gone, she decided sniffily. She waited around for no man! Feeling furious with him and, for no reason, the whole male population, Avena picked up her weekend case and went to bed.

She had cooled down a little by Monday morning. 'There was a phone call for you on Saturday,' Mrs Parsons mentioned when she went into the kitchen. 'It was a man, but he didn't leave his name or any message.'

Avena thanked her, glad that it had been Mrs Parsons who had taken the call. Had it been her mother she knew that she would have heard a good deal more about it.

She drove herself to work, seeming unable to get Nyall Lancaster out of her head, and found that she was beginning to wonder if she had been a little bit hasty. Nyall had phoned twice, after all.

By evening she was feeling restless and, her mother out, she browsed through the bookcase for something that might absorb her attention. She'd read almost everything, she realised, but pulled out a slim volume on flowers and their language which her grandmother had left behind.

She browsed through it for a minute or so, read about the purple hyacinth and went on, but then went back. Purple hyacinth meant sorrow, she re-read, and hesitated. Observing that there was an illustration of the flower, she thought for a while and then went and gathered together some sketching materials and her water-colours and, hoping to relieve her feeling of restlessness, set to work on drawing and then painting a purple hyacinth.

She had always had a flair with water-colours but when the card she created turned out much better than she had hoped she hesitated again.

By morning her painting was dry. Should she? Should she not? She stopped dithering, found a pen and inside the card wrote, 'Apologies, big bad wolf—I went to my grandmother's.' She didn't sign it. If he didn't know who it was from, tough. She found an envelope, wrote 'Personal' across the top, then, looking up Nyall's business address in the phone book, addressed it to him and put a stamp on it.

She stopped by a postbox on her way to work, went through another bout of should she, shouldn't she, and, in a moment of impatience with herself, let it fall from her hands into the waiting slot—too late then to change her mind. He should receive it the next day.

Avena stayed home the following evening—not that she expected Nyall to ring. He didn't. The next day, Thursday, her friend Kate rang her at her office suggesting a game of tennis after work.

'Love to,' Avena accepted, and went home that evening to find that there was a letter for her on the hall table.

In point of fact, it was a card. A hand-painted card illustrating a posy of celandines. Swiftly she looked inside, and promptly started to grin. It was unsigned but the inscribed 'I'd still like to eat you all up' in a firm masculine hand said it all.

A smile was still there on her lips as she looked at the painting again. Rather a splendid painting, she saw, but why celandines? Perhaps there was no reason. After all, Nyall couldn't be expected to know that her purple hyacinth had any meaning, could he?

Nevertheless she could not resist going to the bookcase and taking out the book she had copied the hyacinth illustration from. She looked up celandine—and had to laugh again. Celandine, she read, meant joys to come! Cheeky devil. No way.

She went out for her game of tennis in a cheerful frame of mind, came home tired and happy and had the best night's sleep she'd had in some time.

Avena was not expecting Nyall to call the next night when she got in from work but went to answer the phone when it began to ring, ready to take a message for her mother should the call be for her. 'Hello,' she said.

'May I speak with the artist in the house?' Nyall enquired.

A light laugh escaped her. Suddenly she felt alive, excited. 'Did you paint the celandines?' she asked.

'Would that I had such talent—I got one of our illustrators to do them.'

'It's a lovely picture,' she commented, and just had to ask, 'Do you—um—know what they mean?'

'I didn't know if *you* did.'

'Perhaps we've got the same book,' she laughed.

'Could be—I sent my PA searching for one when I had the notion that to paint your hyacinth especially rather than more simply buy any old card might signify some meaning.'

'Still as smart as ever, I see.'

'What can I tell you that you don't already know?' She could hear a smile in his voice. Then he was asking, 'Going to your grandmother's this weekend?'

Her heartbeats quickened. 'Not this weekend,' she replied.

'Any plans?' he asked casually.

'I've a few offers—I'm not sure which one to accept.'

'While I don't doubt that you could date any one of a dozen men this weekend, something tells me you're lying.'

She laughed. 'You bring out the best in me.'

'Sounds promising,' he commented wickedly, but went on seriously, 'I'm looking in on a party tomorrow evening. Care to come?' Avena swallowed, knowing that she would like to go, just as every instinct of self-preservation said that she should not go anywhere with him. 'Come on, woman,' Nyall growled, clearly believing he had waited long enough. 'I came to your function without complaint. The least you can do is come to mine.'

To take him to her 'function' had been her way of getting her own back on him for his audacity in stating that he wanted to bed her, and on her brothers-in-law for daring to think that she would allow herself to be used. But although Nyall had left her with the washing-up, and had gently, but lightly, saluted her mouth with his on parting, he had otherwise behaved impeccably that night.

'Well, if you put it like that...' She bucked her ideas up, realising that Nyall wouldn't wait for her answer much longer. 'What time?' she asked.

'I'll pick you up at seven. We'll have dinner——'

'You never said anything about dinner!'

'After the superb way you fed me, I should let you starve? From there we'll look in on this party and——'

'Is it formal, this party?'

'Go on, ask,' he teased.

Ridiculously, she found that she enjoyed being teased by him. 'What shall I wear?' she complied.

'The little black dress,' he answered. She came off the phone laughing.

By good fortune, even though she was a female who would allow no man to dictate what she should wear, she had a superb black dress in her wardrobe that suited her delicate colouring to perfection. In the circumstances, she could afford to be generous; she would wear it.

'Are you out this evening, Mother?' she asked her parent the following morning.

'Of course. Are you?'

'I've a date,' Avena admitted, but was loath to tell her who with. 'Oh, by the way, Gran wanted to know if it will be all right for her to stay overnight two weeks today. She wants to go from here to the airport on Sunday.'

'She knows she can stay! She doesn't have to ask— she knows that.'

'That's what I said.'

'Provided she doesn't expect me to stay in and entertain her.'

Avena studied her reflection in the mirror that evening and realised that she had forgotten how well her black dress of the finest light wool crêpe became her. For all its straight simplicity it seemed to show her curves to perfection without being overly clinging. It finished just above the knee, causing her to be grateful that she had long, slender legs.

She owned to a feeling of excitement that any minute now she would see Nyall, but wondered, not for the first time, why she was going out with him. He had come to her 'function' because, as he had stated so openly, he wanted her in his bed. So why, when she had no intention whatsoever of getting into his bed, was she going to his 'function'?

It was unanswerable. And then the doorbell sounded, and her heart leapt, and she picked up her evening purse and went to answer it.

'My God,' Nyall murmured as she opened the door to him. 'There are little black dresses and then there are little black dresses.' He paused, looked at her admiringly, and then added, 'You know, of course, that you look sensational.'

Her heart raced. 'For you, I bothered,' she replied impishly, and, because good manners insisted, invited, 'Come and say hello to my mother.' She led the way to the drawing-room—to discover that her mother's charm was out in full force when she knew who her daughter's date for the evening was.

'Nyall!' she exclaimed. 'Avena didn't say——' She broke off, clearly realising that it was not quite nice to intimate that she had thought her daughter's date was with someone else.

'How are you, Mrs Allad——?' he began smoothly.

'Oh, call me Dinah. Everyone does,' she trilled. And to Avena's embarrassment she added, 'I'm so sorry Avena thought to entertain you in the kitchen the other Saturday. She'd given the housekeeper the weekend off, but that really doesn't excuse——'

'It was my suggestion that we eat in the kitchen,' he lied beautifully, and Avena could have kissed him 'It's very pleasant to dine informally sometimes, don't you agree?'

'Oh, yes, indeed,' her mother twittered. But before Avena could feel embarrassed again at her mother's complete turn of face—after the lecture she'd given her too!—Nyall was saying how very pleasant it was to meet her again but that since they were dining early, prior to going on to a party, they'd better get off now.

They were in the car and had turned out of the drive before he glanced at Avena and stated, 'I've an idea you've had something of a rough time one way and another.'

'I can take it,' she smiled.

'I'm sorry,' he said simply.

'Stop trying to soften me up.'

He laughed. 'You realise you're driving me insane.'

Her heart pounded. He was having a peculiar effect on her too. 'Take a cold shower,' she advised.

'Did you know that, according to latest research, a cold shower is a stimulant, not a suppressant?'

'You've just made that up!' she laughingly accused.

She still had mirth about her mouth when a moment later Nyall pulled up at some traffic-lights and turned to look at her. She saw his warm glance on her mouth, saw his look move to take in the fine porcelain of her skin enhanced by her black dress, before he transferred his gaze up to the brilliant blue of her eyes.

'Tell me, Avena,' he began, his expression deadly serious, 'may I hope, since you've opted to wear an outfit of my choice, that it's possible you'll do everything else I ask this evening?'

Her throat dried at his still deadly serious expression. And then she looked into his eyes and laughter bubbled up inside her—those dark, all-seeing eyes were most definitely dancing.

'Not a chance!' she gurgled.

The restaurant where they had their meal was fashionable yet exclusive, and they were afforded every attention. Avena started with a few hors-d'oeuvres, went on to salmon, and ended with cheesecake, but was so busy talking, laughing, asking, answering, dissecting and laughing again with Nyall that she was barely aware of eating.

He was witty, amusing and serious in turn. Yet while she knew he must converse with some of the best brains in the country he listened intently to anything she had to say with seeming interest. He was altogether the most intriguing mixture of a man she had ever met, was able to discourse on any given subject, but still wanted to hear her views. Avena found him heady and fascinating and yet, while she was aware that he was unlike any man she knew, she felt totally at ease and relaxed with him throughout the meal.

'Where is this party?' she asked as they drank coffee. 'I didn't get round to asking.'

'Not far from here,' Nyall replied. 'Though I'm beginning to wonder if I should take you there.'

'You've noticed the way I slurp my soup?'

'I've noticed the way that men here can't keep their eyes off you.'

Her mouth fell slightly open. 'Honestly?' she gasped, having noticed only the way women looked at *him*. 'I wish you'd mentioned it earlier so I could have enjoyed it.'

The corners of his mouth twitched. 'Hussy,' he berated her, and, their coffee finished, added, 'Come on. Against my better judgement, let's party.'

His friends, Bernice and Edward Ford, lived about a half-hour's drive away, and the party was in full swing when Nyall escorted Avena into their palatial home.

'Nyall!' Bernice came over straight away, her husband joining her in no time. Edward stared at Avena as though spellbound as Nyall made the introductions.

'You're too lovely to be loose among this crowd,' he told her gravely. 'You'd better stick close to Nyall this evening.'

Chance would be a fine thing, she thought an hour later. Nyall had introduced her to many people, and at the start had stayed close as people had come over to chat to them. Several times, though, someone had come to ask his advice or request his attention elsewhere.

Not that she lacked attention, for no sooner would he go than there would be a male or two there engaging her in conversation. And, it was true, Nyall was always swiftly back. But ten minutes ago he had been called away again, and while she knew exactly where he was—over there in the corner where a very elegant, willowy brunette was taking a very serious interest in him—he didn't seem to be busting a gut to get away from her.

So Avena smiled and chatted to the two men who had introduced themselves as Guy and Richard and was sure she was not the tiniest bit jealous. Grief, what an absurd idea! In the main they were sophisticated types—it was a sophisticated kind of party. But as Guy and Richard made her laugh by suggesting they would both go into a decline if she didn't give them her phone number she realised that, just as Nyall had taken in his stride her taking him to the village hall concert, she was quite able to cope with the sophisticated party he had brought her to.

'If anybody's getting Avena's phone number it's me.' A man she vaguely remembered being introduced as Brian Goss joined their group. She took the opportunity to take a surreptitious look in Nyall's direction, and saw that a blonde was trying to cut the brunette out.

'Actually, my phone's out of order at the moment,' she dragged her attention back to lie.

'What's your address? I'll be around first thing in the morning to fix it,' said Brian promptly, and she burst out laughing.

'If you're ready...?' Her heart lifted. She hadn't known Nyall was so close; he hadn't stayed near the blonde long.

'You want to leave?'

'If you can tear yourself away.' His mouth was smiling but, astonishingly, as Avena looked up into his eyes she saw that they were positively arctic!

Feeling more than a little shaken, she managed to mask her feelings. Nyall barely gave her time to say goodbye to Richard, Guy and Brian before, with a firm hand on her arm, he was steering her to offer their thanks and adieus to Bernice and Edward, and then, with his hand still on her arm, he was guiding her out to his car.

Without a word he opened the passenger door and barely waited until she was inside before he slammed it shut—she didn't need two guesses to know that something had upset him.

A few seconds later he joined her in the car. Still without a word, he turned on the ignition and headed in the direction of her home. In no time at all, or so it seemed, they had left the built-up area and were on the motorway, and the silence stretched.

They were about to come off the motorway when Avena decided she had had enough. 'I suppose you've heard of the bear-with-a-sore-head syndrome?' she broke the silence to enquire pleasantly, and heard his unamused grunt.

'What does it feel like to have every man in the room ogling you?' he snarled.

Ogling! Any other time she might have laughed. But she had been through the whole gamut of emotion that night—not least the emotions that had stirred when she'd been standing, albeit with other men, while he conversed across the room with glamorous women. And the feeling that roared through her just then was an almost overwhelming one of wanting to hit him.

'Great!' she retorted. 'Absolutely great!'

'You enjoyed it so much?'

'It was wonderful. Thank you so much for taking me.' Damn him to hell!

Silence, a deafening silence, reigned as he steered off the motorway and drove into open country. An angry quiet persisted between them for the next couple of miles, and Avena started to grow angrier than ever. What had she done wrong, for heaven's sake? Absolutely nothing! And yet...

She was well and truly wanting to box his ears when all at once he broke the taut silence, all anger gone, good humour only there as he commented, 'You realise, of course, that I shall never take you to another party?'

'I wouldn't come if you asked!' she fired back loftily, but her sense of humour was again bubbling up to meet his and she could not hold down a splutter of quiet laughter, which of course, Nyall being Nyall, he picked up.

He pulled over and halted the car. It was a dark night and she could only guess that his expression was a smiling one as he turned to her and enquired, 'Are you going to forgive this bear, Goldilocks?'

Was there ever such a man? To stay frosty with him was impossible. Her anger with him seemed never to have been. 'Who could resist you?' she smiled, and afterwards never knew whether it was because of her words, or the fact that they both moved closer to each other—he to kiss her lightly in apology, she to receive his kiss, all being forgiven, no hard feelings—that the light kiss didn't happen.

That was to say it did happen, but what should have been a brief touching of lips somehow got lost the moment she felt his wonderful mouth against hers and he felt the touch of her softly parted lips beneath his.

Suddenly she did not want to pull away, and perhaps when she might have found the strength she discovered that that strength was not needed as, with a murmur of sound, Nyall, releasing them both from their seatbelts, reached for her and gathered her closer to him.

His arms were strong, his shoulders broad, and the control panel of the car between them was as nothing. All she felt was the firm wall of his chest, the delight that his mouth on hers afforded. As he held her she held on to him, returning kiss for kiss, luxuriating in the feel of his lips against the arch of her throat when his mouth left hers and he trailed kisses down, past her throat, to the silken porcelain of the part of her chest exposed by her dress.

She clung on to him when his mouth returned to hers, when he let go of her with one arm and then, pulling back, gently inserted the backs of his long, sensitive fingers to stroke inside the front of her dress. She felt the warmth of his touch smooth from the soft upper swell of one breast to another, and a flame of wanting such as she had never known started to flicker inside her.

Nyall removed his hand from her dress and used that hand to cup the side of her face when, with more passion than she had ever experienced, his mouth met hers again, and she was lost to everything as an emotion she had never known roared to life within her and, frenziedly, she returned his kisses.

How long she was locked in his embrace she never knew, but she was so aware of him—aware of his touch, aware of every tantalising whisper of his hand. But when his hand strayed beneath the front of her dress and inside her bra, and she felt the whisper of his touch tease the hardened peak of one of her breasts, so that desire for him started to make a complete and utter nonsense of all she had ever believed in, alarm bells started to ring.

But it was Nyall who seemed to be calling a halt to their lovemaking, or so she thought when, 'We can't,' he murmured, his voice thick in his throat.

'C-can't?' she stammered, her brain in neutral.

'Not here. Not in a car,' he went on, adding decisively, 'We'll go to my place.'

For long stunned seconds all ability to think deserted her. She felt overwhelmingly tempted. She wanted to go back to his home with him—though not particularly to see his home. He wanted her in his bed—she wanted to be there.

Unhurriedly he slid his fingers back from her upper breast and removed his fingers from the front of her dress, and only then was Avena able to take heed of those alarm bells. His place! Oh, heavens, what was she thinking about?

Nyall bent his head as if to kiss her one more time before he set the car in motion and sped back to his bed but—and she never knew how, when her world was spinning out of control and what she wanted were his kisses—she somehow managed to pull away.

'No!' she gasped with what strength of voice she could find.

'No?'

'W-would you take me home?' she requested, not a bit surprised that her voice came out sounding all wobbly. '*My* home!' she added hastily.

'I got the message the first time.'

She hadn't expected him to sound ecstatic; he didn't. She pulled further away from him. He let her go. She twisted in her seat to face the front and felt a tension so strong emanating from him that for a while she felt sure he would slam the car into gear and speed back to his home anyway.

But he did not. Perhaps ten more seconds passed during which he turned from her and gripped hard on to the steering-wheel. Then swiftly, decisively, he set the car in motion and did not, as she had feared, reverse it and head back to London, but went on the way they had been going.

It was a silent drive back to her home during which Avena could not get over the emotions Nyall had aroused in her, the way she had felt, the way she had wanted him—and still did.

What he was thinking she had no idea, but if she nursed any vague idea that he might lightly kiss her in parting as he had that last time she very soon discovered that Nyall was not even feeling that friendly towards her.

In fact, so unfriendly was he that although when they drew up on her drive he got out of the car and stood looking down at her for a few more moments not so much as a word did he say to her.

On her part Avena was still trying to come to terms with the passionate person his lovemaking had flushed out of her and had nothing to say to him either. She turned from him and went towards her front door. He did not go with her. She found her key and unlocked the door, and heard him set the car in motion.

She entered the house, and heard him drive away. She closed the door and slowly climbed the stairs. She went to bed knowing that it was over—she would never hear from Nyall Lancaster again.

CHAPTER FIVE

AVENA got up on Sunday morning with the fact indelibly imprinted on her brain that anything there had been between her and Nyall was over. From the outset he had stated his aim and, recalling the staggering responses he had been able to arouse in her, he had not been too far off achieving it.

But he had taken her refusal without argument and had delivered her home when she had said that was what she wanted, and she knew it was the end. She had refused to be seduced, though Lord knew from where she'd got that strength! But Nyall had accepted it and would not contact her again.

Not that she would go out with him again if he did ask, she told herself stoutly, searching for some very much needed stiffened backbone. But he wouldn't ring again and, oh, damn, she had never felt so mixed up.

'You're a dark horse,' her mother accused when, up extraordinarily early for a Sunday morning, she joined her in the breakfast-room.

'You mean Nyall.'

'Of course I mean Nyall—why on earth didn't you say that he was your date last night?'

'Well . . .' Avena hedged, and, not liking to be pushed into a corner, decided on the truth. 'Well, I don't mean to be rude, but the last time Nyall called here, Lucille and Coral were here too to form a reception committee.'

Dinah Alladice looked for a moment as if she was going to take exception to her youngest daughter objecting to her ringing her other two daughters on the matter. Then she seemed to think about it for a moment, and changed her mind. 'You're—sensitive about him?' she enquired, and Avena had to think quickly.

She could tell her mother that she was never going to see Nyall again, but that would only elicit a barrage of questions. The way she was feeling just then, any questions about why she and Nyall had terminated their brief friendship would be much too personal to share with her mother—and, through her mother, with Lucille, Coral and Tony and Martin as well.

On the other hand, it could be that if she let her think she was sensitive about Nyall, then her mother might pass that on too, with instructions that if they knew what was good for them they would leave her alone for a while.

'Yes, I am sensitive about him,' she admitted quietly. Tony and Martin didn't deserve any better. And anyhow, it could not be a lie—though perhaps she was more sensitive about their lovemaking, and the heady response Nyall had wreaked in her, than sensitive about him.

Avena had to have financial discussions with her brothers-in-law the next day in connection with the open day they were having a week the following Friday. She was closeted with them for half an hour, but it was at once evident that her mother had been in touch with her sisters for, while it was certain that they knew she had been out with Nyall on Saturday, not one word did they say on the subject; nor did they so much as breathe his name.

That turned out to be the only bonus that week. Somehow she could not work up any enthusiasm for anything. Life, she decided, was particularly dull just now. Even the fact that she took several phone calls at her office from men who had been at the party on Saturday failed to brighten her mood.

'How did you find out where to contact me?' she asked Brian Goss when he rang to ask her to go out with him.

'With a great deal of difficulty,' he answered. 'I knew Nyall wouldn't tell me if I asked——' she doubted that '—so I grilled everybody else at Edward's party on Saturday until I found someone who remembered asking about your job and where you worked. Having come clean on that, are you going to reward my honesty by saying you'll have dinner with me tonight?'

She remembered Brian—slick, sophisticated—and she wasn't interested. In her view he wouldn't be hurt in the slightest if she told him no. 'Sorry, Brian——' she injected a smile into her voice '—I'm not available.'

There was a pause. He took it as she had hoped. 'I shall ring in a few weeks' time,' he promised. 'Don't forget me till then.'

Avena went home on Friday evening feeling slightly cheered that even if Nyall couldn't be bothered to ring—not that she wanted him to, heaven forbid— there were some men who were eager to date her.

The more she thought about it, however, the more she realised that it was clear from Brian Goss's 'I shall ring you in a few weeks' time' that if she *had* been telling him she was not available because she was seeing Nyall, then Brian was certain that a few weeks was all it would last. Damn Nyall Lancaster; she didn't care a jot that the average length of his relationships lasted mere weeks rather than months.

Her mother was out for the evening. Avena ate her meal in solitude and caught herself sighing as she recalled her parting from Nyall last Saturday. He hadn't even wished her goodbye—not that she'd needed to hear it to know that it was all over.

Oh, to the devil with it, what was she sighing over? she fumed angrily. Then the phone rang and she felt like so much jelly. 'Hello,' she said evenly as she picked it up—and heard her friend's ex-husband on the phone in need of someone to talk to.

She came off the phone knowing that she had done herself no favours in agreeing to see Fergus tomorrow evening. Though should Nyall ring, which he wouldn't, it would give her a great deal of pleasure to tell him that she had a date for the evening. Oh, hell, why couldn't she stop thinking about the wretched man?

Saturday evening with Fergus was not the highlight of her week. But she felt sorry for him and was able to tell him how well Kate had been the last time she had seen her.

On Sunday morning Avena had a cup of coffee in the kitchen with Mrs Parsons, and hated herself that she almost asked if there had been any phone calls for her the previous night. Bother it, she wouldn't ask, she wouldn't. Mrs Parsons was always most diligent about passing on that sort of information. And who the dickens was she expecting to ring? Just because Nyall had phoned one Saturday when she had been at Kembury. Oh, to the devil with him.

Monday was a day that minute by minute went by on leaden feet, but as the week progressed, with so much to organise—everyone being roped in for the open day on Friday—time positively flew.

Friday dawned bright and beautiful and Avena went into work early dressed in a newish dress of tailored plain green. It was a classic dress and suited her colouring to perfection.

By ten o'clock the caterers had worked like beavers and everyone else was where they should be and the open day began. It started very slowly, with only a trickle of people there, but at twelve o'clock the place started to buzz and Avena, who like the rest of the staff had been chatting to all and sundry, began to think the event was going to be a success.

She started to relax and when a waiter hovered near and offered her a glass of Buck's Fizz she stretched out a hand towards the tray he was carrying and felt someone, someone tall, come to the side of her.

And the next thing she knew was that her heart was racing like an express train because whoever it was bent down to whisper something in her ear, and as soon as she heard that tone, the words, that low-voiced, 'For a virgin, you sure as hell know how to kiss,' she knew who it was.

Somehow she managed to keep her face straight as she took her glass and thanked the waiter. But a feeling of merriment was playing havoc with her, and she turned and looked at Nyall—and only then, when she looked up into his dark eyes, did she admit to that which had been there to know for almost two weeks now, only she had refused to acknowledge it. She was in love with him!

'I do my best,' she smiled, loved him, loved him, loved him, and fought like crazy to stay on an even keel. If she was going to go to pieces let it be later when he wasn't around, she prayed. Oh, that fabulous mouth, that slightly arched eyebrow as he looked back at her, warmth, admiration only there in his look—not a scrap of hostility that she could see.

'Going to have lunch with me?' he asked casually.

Yes, yes, yes, screamed her heart. Dear heavens, she hadn't seen him for nearly two weeks; she was aching to spend some time with him. 'I'm working,' smiled her 'company' head.

'Foiled again,' Nyall commented, and not looking the least dejected—swine!—he went away to chat to someone else, who just happened to be female and pretty with it.

Avena circled the room, trying to look nonchalant and as if she wasn't making for the rest-room where she could put in an intensive five minutes getting herself back together.

She was feeling nowhere near normal, however, when fifteen minutes later she left the rest-room, did a quick scan round the room, but could not see a sign of Nyall.

Feeling sick inside that he had come and gone, that after spending only a minute with him she had deprived herself of more time with him, she strove valiantly to appear normal.

A waiter hovered with a tray of vol-au-vents. Without appetite, she went through the motions of selecting one, and was instantly all over the place again when, out of nowhere, Nyall was there taking the vol-au-vent from her fingers and placing it back on the tray.

What could she say? 'I wanted that!' was the best she could come up with.

'No, you didn't,' he contradicted. 'It would spoil your lunch.'

Her heart sang. 'I've told you, I'm on duty. I can't——'

'Yes, you can,' he cut in, his eyes on her face, her alive eyes. And all but smirking, she was sure of it, he transferred his glance over to where Tony was standing. 'I've just fixed it with your boss.'

Her eyes followed his. Tony looked back, smiling encouragingly. Avena turned back to Nyall, aware that she should be protesting vigorously—she was a woman with a career, able to make her own decisions about whether she took time off to lunch out—albeit with someone who could be influential in furthering their business.

'You know I shall be expected to charm you,' was the most she could manage by way of protest—a needless protest, she realised as soon as the words were out of her mouth: Nyall already knew the score.

'You don't have to try,' he murmured, and her legs went like jelly. He was not a man who normally said what he did not mean but was he—if she was reading it right and it wasn't just plain wishful thinking—intimating that she could charm him without even trying?

'Ready?' he enquired, and she could find not so much as another breath of protest.

They lunched at his club. The food was good but she was barely aware of what she ate. Nyall was charming and entertaining and it was bliss, pure and simple, just to be with him. As an extra, Nyall seemed to be enjoying her company too.

That was until, as she was tucking into her pudding, he mentioned, 'I bumped into Brian Goss the other day.'

'Oh, yes?'

'You gave him your phone number?'

Avena stared across the table at him. Quite clearly Nyall knew Brian had her phone number. Was he annoyed that at a party he had taken her to she might have given out her phone number to all and sundry? She looked into his dark eyes; they were inscrutable, telling her nothing.

'Somebody at the party must have asked me where I worked.' She had nothing to apologise for, but, because she wanted nothing to spoil this lovely time with Nyall, 'Word must have got around,' she explained.

'Goss wasn't the only one to phone you?' he challenged before she could blink.

Her mouth fell open a little. 'Well, since you ask...' She left it there, not wanting this conversation that was starting to make her feel a little uptight.

'Did you tell the others you were not available too?' he wanted to know.

'Do I pry into your private life?'

'Did you?' He refused to be put off.

'I didn't realise Brian was such a talkative man.'

Nyall shrugged. 'I confirmed you weren't available.'

Her eyes shot wide. 'You let him think I was going out with you?'

'Wasn't it what you wanted him to think?'

She shook her head. 'I wasn't thinking. To say I'm not available is my stock phrase—I didn't mean to imply... It—er—just seems to work most times.' Suddenly she started to object to being pushed into a corner. 'What phrase do you normally use?' she asked coolly, and was severely surveyed by him for all of five equally cool seconds.

Then unexpectedly a light of amusement lit his eyes. 'You're a cheeky bitch, Miss Alladice,' he informed her. She laughed—she couldn't help it—and fell straight into his trap when he lightly enquired, 'Who else rang you?'

'Richard and some man called Nick and——' She broke off, amazed that for the second time he had caught her off guard, and so discovered that which he had every intention of knowing. 'And you, Mr Lancaster, are a cheeky swine.'

His answer was to grin, and then to flick a glance at his watch. 'For you I'd cancel my meeting,' he murmured.

'What sort of a girl do you think I am that I'd let you?' she laughed, knowing that it was over, but that she had this lovely memory to hoard.

'One who would blossom under my tuition, I feel sure,' he suggested.

Oh, the temptation! 'I think you've taught me enough,' she demurred with what little common sense she had that had not been shattered. Heaven help her, Nyall could seduce her without so much as touching her; she felt quite heady. 'I'd better get back to the fray,' she added, and didn't know whether she was glad or sorry when Nyall, knowing as well as she that Tony wouldn't say a word if she didn't go back that afternoon, accepted that she had chosen work rather than anything which he felt like cutting his meeting to do.

He went with her to her offices, but held the taxi as he got out to say goodbye. 'Thank you for lunch,' she said politely, and felt electricity jolt through her when he took hold of her by her upper arms and brought her that much closer to him.

'Bye, love,' he bade her softly, looking deeply into her eyes.

'Bye,' she answered quietly, felt the thistledown lightness of his kiss to her cheek and, working solely on autopilot, turned about and entered Marton Exclusives.

He had called her 'love'! He had kissed her cheek, albeit lightly, but she could still feel it. Avena was very near swooning when, the fact that the open day was still going on passing her by, she went straight to her office. She loved him. Oh, how she loved him.

She was still sitting at her desk at four-thirty, having done very little work, when Tony and Martin came looking for her. 'Nice lunch?' Tony enquired, and asked no more than that. Which told her that while both he and Martin were, as ever, wildly anxious to know what, if anything, had been said about Marton Exclusives and if she had put in a plug for them, they were still—thanks to her mother's intervention— backing off.

'Lovely, thank you,' she responded, and only just managed to hold down the remark that she hadn't known he had sent Nyall Lancaster an invitation. Somehow she did not want to discuss Nyall with them. 'How's it gone—the open day?' she asked instead.

She drove herself home that evening in something of a dream. She had today admitted to herself that she was in love with Nyall, and, although she knew that there was no future in that love, it was new love, a love she had never experienced before—an emotion she found shattering—and it took some getting used to.

'Are you all right?' her mother enquired sharply midway through their evening meal.

Avena rapidly snapped out of her trance—of recalling how wonderful those shared hours with Nyall had been at lunchtime. 'Yes, of course,' she answered brightly. 'Why?'

'That's twice I've asked you if it's tomorrow that your grandmother arrives.'

'Oh, sorry. Yes, it is. Mrs Parsons has prepared a room and made a bed up for her—despite my saying I'd do it.' She put in a good word for the housekeeper she was still hopeful would beat the duration for housekeepers record in her home.

'Why on earth should you do it when she's perfectly capable, not to mention paid to do such work?'

Avena opened her mouth, and then closed it. Her mother would never understand that her grandmother's arrival, for all she was a pleasure to have around and no trouble at all, still meant extra work for Mrs Parsons.

Her mother stayed in that evening and they watched some television. That was to say Avena found that to sit staring at the television screen was quite a good way of being seemingly absorbed in watching something while she gave her mind over to the wonder that, if asked, she would have said that Nyall Lancaster was just not the type of man she would fall for, but . . . she had gone and done exactly that.

It was true, though, that until she had got to know him a little she had on sight labelled him sophisticated, a man to avoid. And then she had met him, found he could enjoy the unsophisticated, discovered he could, without effort, make her laugh and make her want to be with him. He had kissed her—and turned her nice sensible world upside-down. So how come it had taken until today for her to face up to the fact that she loved him?

'This is rubbish!' her mother pronounced of some film they had supposedly both been watching. 'I'm going to bed.'

'I'll switch it off and do the same,' Avena answered with relief. At last she was able to go to her room without her mother wondering why, so early, she should want to hide away.

She awoke many times that night and was awake early. It was daylight. She got up, was restless, so went and took a shower. It was still early when, dressed in jeans and a T-shirt, her bed made, her room tidied, she went down the stairs and into the kitchen.

She was drinking a cup of tea when Mrs Parsons came and joined her and allowed her to make a fresh pot of tea. She would not allow her to join her for breakfast, however, and Avena, who had realised that the housekeeper liked matters just so, agreed to take her breakfast in the breakfast-room.

It was still only eight o'clock when, having finished what little breakfast she wanted, Avena put down her napkin and the phone rang. Instantly her mind went to the man who was already occupying her thoughts.

Stupido, she scoffed, and went to answer it, praying that it was a wrong number; she just wasn't up to a basinful of Fergus tonight. She picked up the receiver, realising that she had a tailor-made excuse for not going out with Fergus should it be him—her grandmother was coming to stay overnight. Though why Fergus would ring her at this early hour... 'Hello?' she enquired, and all but lapsed into heart failure.

'Good morning, Avena,' Nyall greeted her.

'Oh, hello,' she replied, and, in the absence of anything more brilliant, asked, 'Couldn't you sleep?' As if she should be witty at eight o'clock in the morning!

'Did I wake you?'

'Oh, no, I've been up ages,' she trotted out in a rush—and could have groaned aloud. Now he knew that *she* was the one who couldn't sleep. Naturally the man hadn't got to be where he was by being a lie-abed. 'I've always been an early riser,' she thought to inform him lest he should suspect that thoughts of him, restless thoughts of him, were keeping her from her sleep. Grief, get yourself together, girl! she told herself. 'Did I leave my umbrella in the taxi?' she enquired, knowing as well as he that, yesterday having been a lovely sunny day, she hadn't had an umbrella with her.

'What am I going to do with you?' he replied, amusement there in his voice. How about staying and talking to me all day? she wanted to plead.

'You could try telling me why you've rung before we've taken the milk in,' was what in fact she did answer.

'Well, since you ask,' he complied, 'it occurred to me that if you're joining me here for dinner this evening I'd better get on to arranging a chef.'

Dinner with him? 'Here'? Did he mean his apartment? Her head swam.

'Er—where's "here"?' She fought for sense as she sought clarification.

'My place,' he replied lightly.

'You're not serious?' Yes, yes, yes, I'll come, I'll come.

'Nothing will happen that you don't want to happen,' he assured her.

Oh, help. She knew she could trust what he said. What she could not trust, she now knew, was herself. She took a deep breath and steadied herself to tell him no, she was declining his invitation. 'I come home after pudding?' she heard her treacherous self ask.

He gave an exaggerated sigh and she wanted to laugh. 'If you insist,' he said heavily.

She did laugh; she couldn't help it. 'You could dine here,' she invited, realised that wasn't what she wanted, and added hastily, 'My family would love it.'

'Your family still giving you pressure?' Nyall asked abruptly, all sign of amusement suddenly gone.

'They're not actually,' she replied honestly, wanting him to be good-humoured again. 'But you'd be quite a catch,' she told him, hoping for a smile at least.

'Only I'm still running and marriage scares you to death.'

'I'm not scared,' she stated. 'I just know what it is I don't want,' she tacked on, glad she could be so open with him.

'Marrying money is out,' he stated in turn, surprising her that he'd remembered. He paused for a moment, and, good humour back in his voice, she was glad to hear, added, 'Since this moneyed man isn't asking, you've got nothing to worry about,' and informed her, 'I'll call for you at seven.' And that was it.

Avena put down the phone hoping that Nyall was right and that she did have nothing to worry about.

He had stated at the outset that he wanted her in his bed but, even though his bedroom couldn't be a mile away from his dining-room, nothing would stop her from going to his apartment for dinner that evening. For now, an urgent inspection of her wardrobe was called for.

After a process of elimination—too sophisticated, too unsophisticated, too smart, too simple—Avena finally decided that a loose-fitting trouser-suit of pale green silk, with its cream silk green-edged camisole, was about right for the occasion and, having got the anxiety of what to wear out of the way, she suddenly remembered—her grandmother!

Oh, Lord! Her mother was going out for the evening. She couldn't possibly leave the dear love in on her own. Oh, darn it! How could she have forgotten so completely about her like that? How? Love had sent her brainless, that was how!

Reluctantly Avena went and picked up the phone in her room. She would have to tell Nyall that she couldn't come. She had only half dialled his number, though, when she had a sudden idea—and promptly put the phone down again. Perhaps Nyall would dine here, with her and her grandmother. Perhaps he wouldn't, she realised a moment later. She had put that invitation to him when he'd phoned and although she had not actually withdrawn it he had refused without in fact saying so with his 'I'll call for you at seven'.

Avena dialled again, rehearsed what she had to say in the time it took for him to answer and, when the phone was answered, discovered, with no small degree of astonishment, that she had dialled a Kembury number!

'Hello?' answered her grandmother in her sweet and pleasant voice.

'Gran?' Avena queried, scarcely able to believe that she, level-headed she, had suddenly become so addle-pated.

'Hello, dear,' her grandmother answered. 'I've been meaning to ring you for a couple of days now but I've been so busy...'

'You're all right? You're still going on holiday?'

'I'm fine, and nothing will stop me from taking that plane tomorrow,' she replied, to Avena's relief. 'It's just that I rang Irene Vine the other day—you remember Irene; she lives in Monks Cottages about half a mile from you.'

'You were quite friendly with her when you lived here,' Avena recalled.

'That's right. She's a lovely person—a bit too gullible perhaps. Anyhow, I rang her, told her I'd be with you overnight, and she's kindly invited me to supper tonight. I meant to ring and ask you if you'd mind—I knew your mother wouldn't!'

'Oh, sweetheart,' Avena laughed. 'You're wonderful.'

She came off the phone a few minutes later feeling excited once more at the prospect of seeing Nyall again that evening, and wondering if it was that she had grown addle-pated or if it was Freudian that she had meant to ring Nyall to cry off but had in fact rung her grandmother. And she wondered if, had not her grandmother at once said she was going out she would have somehow, from her love for Nyall, got round to finding out if her dear relative would have minded staying in on her own. She did not think so, but this love she had for Nyall was making a nonsense of her and everything she thought she was.

Her grandmother arrived just after three, and Avena had just settled her in the drawing-room with a tray of tea and scones when her mother appeared out of nowhere. Avena went to collect another cup and saucer and returned to hear her mother enquire, 'You won't mind if I go out this evening? It's a long-stand-ing——'

'As it happens, I've plans of my own,' Grand-mother Carstairs cut in, and turned to Avena. 'You didn't say if you minded, Avena.'

'She probably has plans of her own,' Dinah Alladice put in tartly, and suddenly Avena was embarrassingly conscious of two pairs of eyes boring into her; she was not sure that she did not go a little pink. Whatever, she must have looked a tinge uneasy be-cause her mother's tone abruptly changed, and pleasantly she asked, 'Have you, dear?'

'Um—yes, actually,' she had to confess.

'From the look of you, I'd guess it isn't Fergus,' her mother hinted coyly.

'New man, Avena?' her grandmother enquired gently.

'If it's who I think it is, Avena's sensitive about him,' her mother put in.

'Then we won't talk about him,' Grandmother Carstairs, dear soul that she was, came in swiftly. 'May I have another scone, Dinah?'

When later Avena went up to her room to get ready, she had learned that her grandmother was expected at Irene Vine's around seven and that her mother would be going out at seven-thirty. Which meant that, since Irene Vine's cottage was only minutes away by car, both her mother and grandmother would most likely be there when Nyall called for her.

She owned to butterflies in her tummy when, having showered and washed her hair, she began drying the long golden tresses and suddenly had a mental picture of Nyall that first time she had spoken with him. 'As becoming as it is,' he had said, 'I should like to see you with your hair out of that knot.' Oh, grief. Did having one's hair in a plait constitute 'out of that knot'? This love thing was murder!

When, at six forty-five, Avena left her room, she knew she looked good. Her loose-fitting trouser-suit hinted at her curves, but she hoped not at how her bosom beneath the low-necked camisole pounded. The pale green of her suit set her colouring off to perfection, the rich gold of her hair a superb counterbalance. For once in her adult life, she had left her hair loose. Its long shiny gold ended halfway down her back.

'Avena!' her grandmother exclaimed. 'My dear, you look absolutely sensational!'

Avena was feeling so shaky inside—soon she would see Nyall—that even though 'sensational' was not one of her grandmother's normal words she was glad to hear it. 'Thanks, Gran,' she smiled, and was about to make some light remark about her wearing her rose-coloured glasses when she realised from the car keys in her grandmother's hand that she would soon be leaving for Irene Vine's. 'Can you hang on to meet Nyall?' she asked. 'He——'

'Ah! It *is* Nyall, then,' her mother declared triumphantly, and just then the doorbell sounded.

'I—I'll go!' Avena escaped. The grandfather clock in the hall said that there were five minutes to spare before Nyall was due. But, since he'd come some distance and she didn't expect him to be accurate to the second, she hoped it was him.

She opened the door; it was him. Her heart went into overdrive and just as she was suddenly struck dumb so Nyall, his glance going over her, seemed totally speechless. Then he was stretching out a hand and touching the shining golden hair about her face, and, 'Oh, Avena Alladice, child of a Monday,' he breathed, 'fair of face is just not good enough!'

She wanted to say something, to reply, hopefully with something clever, but her throat felt locked and she did not trust herself to speak. She stood back from the door, studied the hall table for a brief moment. Then her throat unlocked and she invited brightly, 'Come in and meet my grandmother.'

They did not stay long. Avena introduced Nyall to her very comely grandmother who, in her granddaughter's interests, observed him severely for a few seconds, then smiled and with natural charm conversed for a short while.

'My grandmother has an appointment herself shortly,' Avena mentioned as a precursor to their taking their leave.

'Can we give you a lift?' Nyall at once offered.

'I have my own car,' her grandmother smilingly replied.

'The Metro?' he enquired, obviously having noticed the rattletrap of a car which Ursula Carstairs would not part with for love nor money.

'You left it on the front drive?' Dinah Alladice said faintly, and Avena did not miss the gleam of utter enjoyment in her wicked grandmother's eyes.

'It seemed the easiest,' she answered sweetly. 'And now I must be off.'

The three of them went outside together, and Avena and Nyall stood on the drive watching as her grandmother roared away to keep her appointment. They stayed until she turned at the gates and drove out of sight.

'Are all your family beautiful?' Nyall enquired conversationally as he opened the passenger door.

Avena looked up at him, laughter in her eyes. 'We wouldn't have it any other way,' she replied demurely—and thought her heart would stop when, as if he couldn't resist it, he stared down at her impudent expression for a moment, and then bent and placed a light kiss on the corner of her mouth.

Avena was glad to get into the car and feel the car seat beneath her. Oh, heavens, did he know what he could do to her?

She had very little to say on the first part of the drive to his home, but realised that for a man to have such knowledge that he could suggest, as he had once, that she wear her 'little black dress' must mean that he knew a considerable amount about women. She felt that she was not the first woman to fall in love with him, and panicked a little that perhaps he knew the signs. Oh, Lord, she was going to have to watch herself. Pride alone demanded that not by word nor look should she give away so much as a hint of how very much she cared for him.

All he had done was to drop a kiss on the corner of her mouth, and yet it seemed to take an age before she was all of one piece again. She had the breathing-space she needed, though, in the fact that Nyall did not seem to want to be at all talkative, appearing more intent on concentrating on his driving.

'So who's cooking this evening?' She broke the silence as they came off the motorway. 'I refuse to believe you can cook.'

'I'll have you know I do a very mean eggs on toast,' he retorted.

And she loved him and it wasn't going to show, but she had to allow herself a smile. 'You said something about arranging a chef?'

'Chef and assistant, to be accurate,' he replied. 'Victoria and Stuart—or, to give them their formal title, In-Home Catering—have been popping in on and off for a couple of years and cooking for me.'

So don't think you're anything special, Avena Alladice! But she didn't want to think of the other women he had entertained at his apartment—such thoughts only made her feel sick inside. 'They're that good?' she queried lightly, knowing for sure that In-Home Catering would have to be or they wouldn't get through the door a second time.

'I'll let you tell me afterwards,' he promised.

His apartment was everything she thought it would be. Smart on the outside, elegant and roomy on the inside. He showed her where the bathroom facilities were and Avena left him briefly, not because she particularly needed to wash her hands and comb her hair but more so that she could top up her not-by-word-nor-look attitude.

Nyall had a Martini poured for her when she joined him in his thickly carpeted drawing-room. 'Come and have a chat to Victoria and Stuart,' he suggested and, causing her heart to pound, placed an arm about her shoulders and turned her in the direction of the kitchen.

It was a big kitchen and it was all happening in there. Consequently they did not go in but Nyall made the introductions from the doorway. Victoria was at the sink doing some washing-up while Stuart was doing something artistic-looking with a tomato.

'There's a delicious smell in here,' Avena said appreciatively.

Stuart was handsome. He smiled, his eyes glued to her. 'I hope you're hungry.'

'Starving.' She returned his smile, and felt Nyall turn her about.

'We'll leave you to get on with it,' he remarked, a degree coolly, she felt.

'You're not cross about anything?' she asked when back in the drawing-room and he, still somewhat coolly, she thought, had suggested that she take a seat on one of the several sofas in the room.

He seemed arrested for a moment. 'Are you always this up front?' he wanted to know.

'Up front?'

'Honest, open—if you think it, say it?'

'You *are* cross,' she decided.

'Who wouldn't be?' he answered wryly. 'I refused to take you to another party because of the mayhem you cause with the male population, and overlooked completely the fact that Stuart was going to be bowled over.'

'Don't be daft! He's got Victoria, and——'

'Victoria's his sister.'

'Ah!' she exclaimed, and was stumped—and then grinned. 'Do you reckon that if I play my cards right—he'd cook for me?'

'Ye gods, you've got a nerve!' Nyall retorted, but, as she had hoped, his lips twitched.

Just at that moment, the moment of her heart turning cartwheels in case there was the tiniest chance that Nyall might be the smallest fraction jealous that other men looked at her, Victoria came in to tell him that dinner was ready.

Avena went with him to the similarly elegant dining-room and, realising how ridiculous she was being to think for so much as a moment that Nyall might be the least bit jealous, could not help but be glad that there were other people in the apartment. She needed to keep her head together; she thought she stood more of a chance of doing that if, while not actually in the same room, there were other people present.

Nyall seated her opposite him at the highly polished antique table. Their starter was a most delicious smoked salmon mousse and she did her best to concentrate solely on her food, but she was overwhelmingly aware of Nyall. She glanced up; he was watching her. 'Er—if you're wondering why I've left the tomato,' she said of the rose sculpture, feeling choked and in desperate need of saying something—anything, 'it's just too beautiful to eat.'

Nyall looked at her, his admiring dark gaze taking in her flawless skin, the perfect shape of her face. 'I'd like to take a bite of you,' he commented.

'Cannibal!' she laughed, and suddenly felt a whole lot easier.

She was relaxed and chatting happily away when Stuart, his handsome look pinned on her, came in and asked if everything was satisfactory. 'I've never tasted better,' she smiled, and saw that he looked delighted.

Shortly afterwards Victoria came in and cleared the first course, and Stuart came back and served the second course. He beamed at her. The lamb fillet and rosemary with a complementary wine sauce and vegetables looked fantastic; he was doing an excellent job. She smiled back. 'This looks delicious,' she offered warmly.

Nyall had been conversing easily too, she had thought, but, perhaps because she was overly sensitive where he was concerned, she started to form the impression, as Victoria cleared yet another delicious course and Stuart served a light, mouth-refreshing green salad with a superb dressing, that Nyall was the merest degree uptight about something.

She became convinced of it a few seconds later when, conversation between them having hitherto flowed unstiltedly, he seemed slightly abstracted. She stopped eating and looked directly at him. He wasn't eating either, and returned her direct look with one of his own that held perhaps a hint of enquiry.

He had asked if she was always this up front. She rather supposed she must be, because there was no way she could hide or ignore that nebulous sort of feeling that something was a speck amiss.

'The food is superb, and my mother has seen to it that no one has better table manners than I—so what's wrong?' she just could not duck from asking.

'My God, you're incredible!' he answered, appearing slightly surprised. His look softened. 'And incredibly sensitive.'

Her heart pounded—he sounded as if he liked that about her. At any rate, he had not picked up why she was sensitive—about him. 'So what did I do?' she asked quietly.

'You? Nothing. And I'm being an exceedingly bad host.'

'You know you're not.'

He studied her, his gaze steady on her. 'You, Avena Alladice, are something else,' he murmured—she thought appreciatively, but managed to keep her eyes fixed to his as she waited to hear what she wanted to know.

'So?' she invited.

His mouth quirked up at one corner—and she loved him. 'So,' he began, 'I'm doing my level best to find it amusing that, though it's Victoria who always does the clearing away and waiting, her brother keeps coming in.'

She stared at him, searching for comprehension. 'You think he's suddenly taken a fancy to the décor of your dining-room?'

'He's take one hell of a fancy to you,' Nyall tossed back at her. And as her eyes shot wide he informed her, 'He keeps coming in to see you.'

'He doesn't!' she denied.

'Would I lie?'

'My word——' She broke off, still not believing it. 'I'm sure you've got it all wrong,' she decided. 'Stuart probably has everything in the kitchen sorted to his satisfaction and, with time on his hands, thought to help his sister.'

Nyall leaned back in his chair. 'You've no idea of the effect you have on some men, have you?' he asked quietly. She did not miss that 'some men', which left him neatly excluded. 'He took one look at you and keeps coming in to feast his eyes on you.'

'No,' she pooh-poohed the idea. 'You'll be saying next that I'm the only passingly pretty female you've

brought here——' She broke off. Nyall was looking
steadily at her again.

'You're the only beautiful woman I've brought here
to dine,' he stated, and Avena suddenly felt way, way
out of her depth.

No doubt many had stayed to breakfast. She took
a gasp of breath—she wasn't happy with such
thoughts. 'I...' she said chokily, but, with Nyall's gaze
fixed firmly on her as he waited for her to go on,
barely knew how to proceed—they seemed to have
gone a long way from Stuart and his sudden penchant
for coming in and interrupting. Stuart no longer
seemed the issue. 'I'm—er—trying the hardest I know
to be sophisticated—um—worldly-wise—but I think
I'm in a little over my head here,' she confessed, and
suddenly felt gauche in the extreme.

But she had no need to worry that she might need
to explain further—that Nyall had not caught her
drift—for he was every bit as astute as she had thought
him and, a hint of a smile there in his voice, he teased,
'You think I'm going to throw you over my shoulder
and sprint with you to my bedroom?'

The picture he conjured up made her smile, and
feel better. 'I—er—think you're loads more subtle
than that,' she replied seriously.

'For that I thank you,' he drawled, but was totally
serious when he added, 'I've told you, love, nothing's
going to happen that you don't want to happen.'

She felt weak at the knees and was glad that her
legs were under the table. All at once she no longer
knew what she wanted. 'For that,' she tossed back at
him with all the impishness she could find, '*I*
thank *you*!'

'Is your grandmother staying with you?' he enquired before she could draw another breath, and, to her relief, they were off the subject which he had plainly observed she felt uncomfortable with.

She felt relaxed once more as she explained about her grandmother going on holiday in the morning. And from there they conversed about various holidays they had both taken then Victoria was there to clear away again and Stuart came in to serve a tasty fruit and filo pastry pudding. But this time, because of Nyall's previous comments, Avena did notice that Stuart seemed to be a little taken with her.

She thanked Stuart politely and told him the sweet looked scrumptious, then avoided eye contact and he went back to the kitchen. Then it was that she glanced across the table to Nyall and saw that, instead of looking uptight as she had half thought he might, there was definitely a look in those dark eyes that plainly said 'I told you so'. She poked her tongue out at him, and he laughed at her sauce, and she loved him.

That was when her emotions started to get out of control. A short while after that Nyall was telling Stuart that they would serve themselves with coffee if he'd like to take it to the drawing-room.

'That was a fabulous meal,' Avena said as she and Nyall left the dining-room. And shortly after that, all clearing away in the kitchen attended to, apparently, Victoria and her brother came into the drawing-room to say that they were leaving. 'That was the best meal I've had in an age,' she thanked them, and wished them goodnight, but as Nyall went to let them out and secure the door she realised that he wasn't the one who was uptight this time—it was she.

'More coffee?' he suggested, coming back and taking a seat beside her on one of the soft, squashy sofas.

'N-no, thanks,' she replied stiltedly, overwhelmingly conscious that, with Victoria and Stuart gone, she was alone with Nyall in his apartment, and that she loved him, and that not by word or look must she give that away. 'Would you excuse me?' she said in an abrupt burst of sound. Suddenly she was panicking and knew a desperate need to be by herself; she quite desperately needed to get herself together.

She didn't look at him again but, aware that he had risen when she had, she went straight to the bathroom, realising as she gave herself another lecture that this facet of being in love—this wanting with everything she had to be with Nyall but terrified she might give herself away—was dreadfully wearing.

Be natural, she instructed herself when she finally left her sanctuary. She entered the drawing-room and saw Nyall still standing where she had left him. *Try* to be natural, she hastily amended her instructions when her insides went all shaky again on just seeing him.

She moved further into the room, and then observed from his expression that he didn't seem too thrilled with her hasty rush to get away from him. 'I'd better take you home,' he clipped.

She didn't want him like this with her: cool, stern. Nor did she want to go. Oh, what an idiot she was. 'Home?' she queried unhappily.

'It's where you live. It's obviously where you feel more comfortable,' he stated, and Avena realised then what but for panic she should have realised earlier—

that Nyall was too smart not to notice she had been on edge.

'Oh, Nyall,' she mourned. 'I'm sorry.' And suddenly she began to feel ashamed. And where before she had had to instruct herself to be natural with him she all at once no longer had to try. In her contrition, it seemed the most natural thing in the world to take those few steps further to him and, as he had earlier planted a light kiss on her mouth, it seemed so natural to place her hands on his waist and stretch up and plant a kiss on the corner of his mouth.

Then she gave a short gasp of breath because, her kiss given and received, she just did not seem able to let go of him, to take her hands away from his waist and step back! She stared up at him as if perhaps hoping he would push her away.

But he did not push her away. Instead, almost involuntarily, it seemed, he slowly gathered her into his arms. To her relief she saw that she was forgiven, saw that all scrap of sternness had gone from him when softly he murmured, 'Oh, Avena, you shouldn't have done that.' And gently, unhurriedly, his head came down, and his lips claimed hers.

As his arms were around her, so her arms went around him. As Nyall broke that gentle kiss, she knew one kiss was not enough. She didn't want him to put her away from him and take her home. She wanted more.

He looked deep into her eyes; she had an idea her eyes were inviting him to kiss her again. Her lips parted and a small groan of sound escaped him, and then those strong, powerful arms about her were pulling her more firmly to him and he was accepting the invitation of her lips.

And, as kiss after kiss Nyall gave and took, Avena began to experience again the upward spiralling of passionate emotion which he had aroused in her before. And she gloried in it. She pressed closer to him, heard a sound—a groan of wanting—leave him, and gloried some more when he slipped her jacket from her shoulders, caressed her back, causing her to clutch on to him tightly, and she felt the warmth of his hands beneath the flimsy camisole top she wore.

He seemed to hesitate, though, as if her suddenly clutching on to him like that had reminded him of her inexperience, and Avena was in panic once more— this time in case her involuntary movement had put him off.

She kissed him warmly, more ardently, and, acting solely on instinct, she pressed her body against him— and Nyall, after only the briefest hesitation, took over. She felt his hands on the silken skin of her back, felt his sensuous caressing up to her bra, and, her bra undone, revelled in the heady sensation of his hands roving where they would over her back.

She tensed, but only slightly, when those wonderful seeking hands caressed the front of her. But it was a gasp of pure pleasure that left her when gently, un-hurriedly, his exploring hands captured and cupped her breasts—naked beneath her camisole.

'Oh, Nyall!' she gasped, his sensitive fingers sending her mindless as they played tenderly over the hardened peaks he had created.

'Oh, Avena, girl. I want you,' he responded, and as he released her breasts so that he could hold her tight and bury his head in the luxurious cloud of her rich golden hair Avena could not deny the fire of wanting he had aroused in her. Never had she felt like this—hadn't known that she could.

'I—er. . .' she murmured huskily, her whole skin feeling alive, scorched.

'You—er?' Nyall queried as her whisper of a voice faded. But she could not answer. She felt far too emotional to be able to utter another syllable.

But so badly did she wish that she had because, all of a sudden, whatever it was Nyall had read from her 'I—er. . .', he was giving her a choice. And she did not want that choice—she just wanted him to take her; she didn't want to think about it.

But she was having to think about it because, quite unexpectedly, he was reminding her, 'Little darling, I've said that nothing is going to happen this evening that you don't want to happen. But you've got to decide, and decide now, because if you don't take your arms from around me and walk to the door, then, sweetheart, I won't be able to let you go until morning.'

Stay until morning? Oh, what bliss! Avena stirred in his arms, intending to press closer still and to let that movement be her answer.

Then, shatteringly, with that word 'morning' floating about in her head, she remembered that, regardless of her grandmother's refusal, she had intended to take her to the airport early the next day. Swiftly on the heels of that thought chased the realisation that if she was not about when her grandmother was ready to leave her grandmother would pop her head round her bedroom door to say goodbye to her.

All Avena knew in that moment of passionately heightened emotions was that there was no way she could allow her grandmother to enter her bedroom and to see that, whoever's bed she had slept in that night, it had not been her own.

From where she got the strength Avena never knew, but that movement towards Nyall never got made. And she was too agitated when she made a move to back out of his arms to think of hanging about to look for her jacket. Too scared she might yet stay— until Nyall, after a tense moment of holding on to her, let her go. Swiftly she went to the door of his apartment.

Her heart, her passion of feeling for him, was yet making a nonsense of her, but with some distance between them she gained sufficient brainpower to do up her bra. But she still had her back to him when, what seemed an age later, he came and joined her by the door and dropped her jacket over her shoulders.

Without a word they left his apartment, and, wanting him, needing him, she was in his car and being driven back to her home before a little more brainpower arrived and she suddenly realised that she need not have taken Nyall so literally. He had said that he would not have been able to let her go until morning, but they could have loved together, and lain together for a few hours, and she could still have been home in time to drive Gran to the airport.

It was too late now, and the nearer they got to her home, the more confused she became over whether she was glad or sorry. Nyall had said nothing throughout the whole duration of the drive, and she rather gathered that he would not welcome any comment from her, so stayed silent.

She had begun to think, as he turned into her drive and steered up to her door, that he might take his leave without another word. But, to her relief, he got out of the car and stood by the entrance of her home with her and, raising a hand, gave a lock of her hair a gentle tug. 'What does it feel like to drive a man mad with desire and then say no?' he enquired evenly.

Oh, Nyall, I love you so. 'I didn't mean to,' she just had to tell him, just as, because she loved him so, she had to add, 'If it's any consolation, I've—um—never felt that sort of—er—chemistry with a man before.'

'Now she tells me!' he complained teasingly, and as her heart filled with joy that they were still friends he growled, 'Go in now before I drive off with you and make you mine!'

She laughed. He bent his head. Their lips met briefly. 'Goodnight,' he said, and abruptly strode to his car.

'Goodnight,' she whispered, and went indoors.

CHAPTER SIX

HER alarm went off long before she was ready for it the next morning. Avena opened her eyes and even while she was wondering why she had set her alarm so early on a Sunday morning Nyall was in her head.

Nyall, Nyall, wonderful Nyall. With some vague recollection stirring that she had set her alarm because she intended driving her grandmother to the airport, Avena got out of bed and showered. Oh, Nyall. Was he still asleep, or was he awake too?

Her grandmother was already dressed and ready when Avena went downstairs. 'What are you doing up?' her grandmother questioned, looking pleased to see her nevertheless.

'You didn't really think I'd let you go without coming to see you off at the airport, did you?' Avena laughed, but added seriously, 'Will you hurry back? It won't be the same knowing you're not at the other end of a phone call to Kembury.'

They shared a sketchy breakfast together—all that they wanted—and Avena thought her grandmother was showing remarkable restraint. But it was as they were driving to the airport that it seemed she could constrain her curiosity no longer, and asked, 'Is he special, this one?'

Avena had no need to ask what she was talking about. Nor could she lie to her. 'He is, Gran,' she admitted quietly, and had never loved her grandmother more than when she just squeezed her hand on the steering-wheel and, instead of asking questions, proceeded to tell her how her evening with Irene Vine had gone.

After she had hugged and kissed and waved her grandmother goodbye, Avena returned to her car and positively sped home. For a Sunday it was still comparatively early, but it had only been eight o'clock when Nyall had phoned yesterday.

On arriving at her home she went straight to the kitchen, passed a few minutes with Mrs Parsons in idle chit-chat, and then asked casually, 'I don't suppose there were any calls for me while I was out?'

There had been none, and Avena spent the rest of the day within earshot of the phone while at the same time telling herself that this had to stop. In the cold light of day, and as the day stretched, common sense began to prod at her. She wanted Nyall, she could not deny that. She loved him, and from that love she wanted him and wanted to give herself to him, but—realism pushed for a hearing—it would not mean anything to him. And, pride suddenly rearing, she did not think she could live with that.

She went to bed that night wondering why she was punishing herself anyway. The phone had stayed silent all day, so of one thing she could be certain; Nyall wasn't busting a gut to make a conquest of her.

She arose on Monday morning proudly determined that she was not going to be made a conquest of anyway. Good grief, what did he think she was? If he rang she would politely but firmly tell him that she saw little point in going out with him again. If he rang, she...

Fate must have been laughing up her sleeve. Nyall did not ring. All week, and she was never very far from the phone, he did not ring. Fergus rang. And Richard and Guy rang. And, as if to endorse his intimation that the cycle of an affair with Nyall wouldn't last that long and that he now expected her to be available, Brian Goss rang.

She was feeling miffed with men in general, and refused all invitations—even to the extent of hardening her heart against Fergus. Even though she now knew just how painful being unwisely in love could be, she refused, and stayed in—near to the phone.

But, save for her sisters telephoning her mother, the phone stayed quiet over the weekend too. And Avena started to get angry, not only with Nyall Lancaster for the pining-for-his-phone-call wreck he had made her, but angry with herself too. Devil take it, what was she that some Casanova of a man could do this to her?

By Wednesday, even when she knew in her heart of hearts that Nyall was not going to ring now, she, with her pride's help, was determined she would tell him to get lost if he did ring. When, that afternoon, a persistent Brian Goss phoned and asked her to have dinner with him she opened her mouth to say no, then thought, Dammit! 'I'd love to,' she answered, and he nearly fell over backwards from shock.

She was not looking forward to the evening but, having accepted, she did her best to be a good companion, and found it went much better than she had anticipated. Brian wasn't Nyall, but he was nicer than she had thought, and although she had to put him firmly in his place when he thought, in the pitch-black of night, to pull up to show her a local beauty spot he took it well. He at once seemed to realise that she was different in this respect from the women he often

went out with, and took on board that he had two
choices—take it or leave it.

He chose to take it. 'If I promise to behave—well,
within certain limits,' he qualified, 'will you come out
with me again?'

She was starting to like him, and besides, she
wouldn't mind making herself scarce at home at the
moment. Her mother had started to forget she was
sensitive about Nyall and two days ago had begun an
increasing campaign of questions, all probing, to find
out why she hadn't been out with him lately. 'Yes, I
will,' she told Brian.

'Fantastic!' he exclaimed, and snatched a quick kiss
anyway. Her father had once had an over-excited
Labrador much like him. 'There's a party on Friday,'
he went on enthusiastically.

She was off parties. At the last party she had been
to she had been with Nyall—dear heaven, would that
man forever haunt her? She had no intention, since
Brian seemed to know some of the same people as
Nyall, of putting herself anywhere near Nyall's orbit.

'I'm busy Friday,' she invented, love making a liar
of her.

'Saturday, then. I could get tickets for the theatre…'

'Fine,' she smiled, and that night went to bed trying
to whip up enthusiasm for Saturday while at the same
time proudly insisting—where once she had seen
nothing wrong in staying at home on a Saturday
evening—that she'd be darned if she'd stay in while
Nyall Lancaster was out on the town.

He was out on the town too! She saw him! For all
her evasive action in refusing to go to the party the
night before, she saw him. Not at the theatre, which

was passably good but which, perhaps because the dratted man was so much in her head, she was not able to give full attention.

'It's too early to take you home yet,' Brian announced as they left the theatre.

'What do you have in mind?' she asked him directly. He was on a hiding to nothing if he said his place.

'No?' he queried, reading her mind.

'No.'

'Nightclub?' he suggested.

Avena thought of how she had not been giving her full attention to the play. Perhaps, in fairness, she owed him. Besides, she was feeling restless. Maybe a nightclub was what she needed.

'Lead on,' she accepted, and smiled.

'You know that your smile drives men nuts?' he queried.

'There's no answer to that,' she laughed, and went with him to a nightclub, and an hour later still felt restless and, she had to own, she had had better times. Why the simple concert at the village hall should spring to mind she had no idea.

Or perhaps she did. It was Nyall, of course. Anywhere with Nyall was exciting, stimulating. Just being with him was uplifting. She caught Brian looking at her, and felt he deserved better. She smiled to let him know that she was enjoying herself.

'Do you come here often?' she enquired for the want of something to say.

'That's my line,' he complained, and they both laughed. And just then she happened to glance over to the door and, with a jolt that juddered through the whole of her, she saw that Nyall Lancaster had just come in!

She glanced hurriedly away, her mind a quagmire while, somehow, she managed to keep a look of well-being on her face. And inside she died. Nyall was not alone. He had the most elegant of blondes hanging on to his arm.

Somehow—through pride, was her best guess—Avena managed to chat about any idle notion that came into her head over the next few minutes. But it was a strain, and she wanted to go home.

'Would you excuse me?' she murmured to Brian. As he was only halfway down his drink, the powder-room seemed an ideal refuge to go and get herself together.

At once he got to his feet, and she rose and made her way through the tables. She had no idea where Nyall was sitting, but she was still feeling dreadful inside about his glamorous companion, and was in no mind to inflict further hurt on herself by trying to spot them.

Avena exited the vast, table-lined room and was in the lobby when, 'You're a long way from home!' barked a voice she would know anywhere, and she stopped dead.

She did not want to turn round. Love, that pig of an emotion, made her do it. She turned, her heart thundering as she looked at him. Tall, dark and, although she didn't want to, even with that icy look on his face she loved him.

'I might say the same thing about you!' she retorted, unsmiling, hoping that what were now shaking limbs would carry her until she'd made it to the powder-room where she could sit down.

'Does Goss know that some girls *don't*?' he enquired toughly, and Avena wanted to hit him; no doubt *his* companion *did*!

'I see you're keeping your hand in!' Jealousy tore the words from her. Oh, God!

'Insolent baggage!' he snarled.

'So sue me!' she flew, did a sharp about-turn and, while she still could, stormed to the powder-room.

Once there she collapsed on to a stool. It wasn't only her legs that were shaking; she was shaking all over. Had he seen that she was jealous? No, he couldn't have. She'd covered it with that snappy 'So sue me!', hadn't she?

Thankfully she had the room to herself for the moment and she did all she could to get herself more of one piece, but she found it extremely difficult. Oh, why had Nyall had to say anything at all to her? And oh, what rotten luck that he had been out in that lobby at the same time.

Or, remembering that he had mentioned Brian and, from what he had said, must have seen her with him, had he come out specially to have a go at her? Her breath caught at that thought; then she remembered how she had thoughtlessly revealed that she had spotted him with his glamorous companion, and wanted to die.

She tortured herself over it for another couple of minutes, and then realised that if she didn't soon get back to Brian he would be sending out a search-party. She left her stool and squared her shoulders.

What the dickens was she grieving for? She had known from the very beginning that she was never likely to be *numero uno* with that arrogant swine for more than a couple of weeks anyway. By her calcu-

lation she had made it a vague hit-and-miss four
weeks—at a stretch, five weeks—and she didn't want
to think about whom he might have dated in between.

She did not see Nyall again that evening. Whether
he was still there or had decided to move on elsewhere, she was determined not to look around to find
out.

'You're very pale; are you all right?' Brian enquired when she got back to him.

It seemed too good an excuse to waste. She almost
invented a headache. 'I wouldn't mind going now,'
she said, leaving it to him to consider that she might
be feeling a little unwell.

Brian Goss was turning out to be far, far nicer than
she had at first believed, and he was instantly concerned and ready to take her home. She hoped with
all she had that Nyall was looking as Brian draped a
caring arm about her shoulders and escorted her out
of there, though she was still not minded to look about
to see if Nyall was still there.

As grateful as she was to Brian, however, she refused his invitation to have dinner with him the next
night. 'I enjoy your company, Brian, but I've other
friends I like to see.' She then felt mean and suggested, 'If you're free next Saturday, I'll take you out
to dinner if you like.'

'You promise not to try to have your wicked way
with me?' he accepted promptly.

Avena kept herself busy in the week that followed.
On Tuesday she went and had a meal with her friend
Kate, and on Wednesday Fergus, seeming to have a
magic eye where his ex-wife was concerned, rang and
during the course of the conversation asked if she had

seen anything of Kate recently. From there he seemed to hit depression again, so that when he said he'd got a couple of tickets for an art exhibition on Friday evening, and didn't want to go on his own, she found herself saying that she'd go with him.

And quite desperately wished she hadn't when, believing at first that she had made a mistake—because she was seeing Nyall in any tall, dark-haired man who happened anywhere near—she discovered that she had not made a mistake and it *was* Nyall. Her eyes were at once drawn to him, Nyall being the first person she saw as she and Fergus entered the gallery!

Her heart set up what was by now a familiar pounding. Then an also familiar sick feeling started to attack—Nyall was not alone. Equally glamorous, but not the blonde this time; he had another elegant female hanging on to his arm.

He had seen her too, but he did not acknowledge her. If anything, he seemed to favour ignoring her! How dared he? Avena tilted her chin at a haughty angle; she loved him and hated him all in the same breath, saw him glance icily at Fergus and was glad, glad, glad that for all that he was as soft as butter inside, and none the worse for that, Fergus was passably good-looking and was built like a rugby lock forward. Nyall flicked an arrogant glance back at her but, with her nose in the air, she walked past him without speaking.

That night, in her bed, she came close to tears. But she wouldn't cry, she wouldn't. The womanising swine wasn't worth it. Out with a different woman each time she saw him! Bubbles to him—she didn't care.

She awoke on Saturday morning knowing that, for all her bravado of last night, she jolly well did care.

She was hurting inside and it just wasn't getting any better.

She spent much of the day fretting that although she and Nyall had conversed about art, so she had known he had an interest in it, she just had not so much as considered that he might be at that art gallery last night. One thing was certain, however. No more art galleries, no more nightclubs. She was keeping well away from his orbit.

'Which beau are you seeing tonight?' her mother asked viperishly when she got up.

Avena nearly said Nyall for the sheer hell of it. 'Brian Goss,' she answered truthfully, and heard a lengthy diatribe on missed opportunities and how her mother didn't know what her poor sisters had done to deserve such selfish treatment.

'Poor sisters?' Avena laughed, in a better position than her mother to know that the firm, with or without her assistance through Nyall with Oakby Trading, was doing very nicely, thank you and that, knowing her sisters, they wouldn't rest until they had their share of the profits.

Avena took Brian Goss to dine at a hotel not too far away from where she lived. But with not a sign of Nyall anywhere, though she had chatted and laughed with Brian, she returned home and went to bed with an ache within her. She missed seeing Nyall. Even when they had passed without speaking she had felt alive.

She had refused Brian's invitation to go out on Wednesday but had agreed to see him on Friday. But, with her mother still badgering her about Nyall, Avena began to wish she had arranged to be out every night that week.

Then just as she had finished her meal on Wednesday evening the phone rang and as she picked it up to answer it she didn't know whether she was glad or sorry that she was home.

'What are you doing tonight?' Nyall asked, and she was instantly alive again, and loving him, and he wasn't going to know that.

'What's the matter? Been stood up?' Who in their right mind would ever stand him up?

'I may have referred to your insolent streak before,' he commented.

'So what else is new?'

'Meet me for a drink?' he floored her by asking.

She almost had her car keys in her hand before a great lump of sanity landed. 'I'm afraid I'm entertaining a... guest at home this evening,' she lied aloofly. And nearly had her ears scorched.

'Who?' he demanded with a snarl.

'That's none of your business!' she retaliated hotly. The sauce of it!

'Since I'm the one who started the thaw in the icy-virgin region, it is my business!' he slammed straight back.

How *dare* he? 'I knew I had to thank you for something!' she hissed. 'I'm having a wonderful time!' she yelled—and didn't know which one of them hurled the phone down first.

She didn't regret it, not a word of it. Who the hell did he think he was that he thought he could pick her up and drop her down whenever it suited him? Meet him for a drink! He could rot in hell! So why was she weeping? Avena angrily brushed tears from her eyes and ran up to her room. She hoped his hair fell out!

She did not sleep well that night. Swine, he'd still be attractive bald. She awoke frequently, and each time it was to go over her conversation with Nyall again. At one point she found that she was weakly considering if she should have gone and met him for a drink. That was when more sanity arrived. Apart from bumping into him those two times, there had been not a peep from him for three and a half weeks, then, as casual as you like, 'Meet me for a drink?' Hanging, drawing and quartering were too good for him!

Avena went to work on Thursday morning tired, exhausted, and still having to bat away the occasional weakness that invaded and said it was all very well proudly to decline his invitation but that all that she had done was deprive herself of seeing him.

By Friday she felt marginally less agitated—or thought she did. She was in the middle of some figure work when she heard her office door open.

'Be with you in a minute,' she acknowledged whoever it was without looking up. Whoever it was seemed to appreciate that she was deeply involved in what she was doing, for kindly he or she said not a word, but stayed silent.

'That's it!' she exclaimed, dropping down her pen, and, looking up, gasped in shock. 'What are *you* doing here?' she asked faintly, that pounding near her ribcage at it again.

Nyall shrugged, clearly in no way as affected to see her as she was to see him. 'I was passing—was almost past, in fact,' he inserted conversationally. 'Then I thought, I know, why don't I pop in and see Avena Alladice—that maiden I stirred to womanhood?'

Oh, grief, she didn't know that she was up to this sort of conversation. Plainly he was referring to her intimation that she had lost her virginity. 'You can tell?' she queried.

'That you've been playing the field?' he rapped toughly.

'Playing the field?' she fired back angrily, on her feet, facing him. Dammit, he was making her sound like some tart.

'You're dating two men at the same time that I know of!' he challenged bluntly.

'Ah!' escaped her. It had never occurred to her before that while she had been fuming about him being a womaniser, out with a different female each time she saw him, each time *he* had seen *her* she herself had been out with a different man. She decided she wasn't happy with this conversation anyway and thought it time to change it. 'Um—did the receptionist show you which was my office?' she queried, off the top of her head.

'If you're thinking of having words with her—don't. Spicer saw me parking my car and came out to say welcome.'

'Tony... Oh, grief! He'll think——' Avena broke off, unable to finish. But Nyall never had been one to shrink from saying something, and finished it for her.

'He'll think that there's something going on between us,' he drawled, and she could have hit him that he could make such a statement—it clearly meaning very little to him.

'Well, he'll just have to realise that there isn't,' she retorted snappily.

She felt her legs go weak when, his expression stern, he demanded, 'Isn't there?'

Oh, heavens, he had no idea what he could do to her. 'Of course there isn't,' she somehow managed to scoff.

'What about the chemistry you feel with me?' he challenged, and she just couldn't handle the subject.

'Er—can I get you a coffee?' she enquired, striving to effect a cool, polite business head and act as if he were any visiting businessman—and could have bitten out her tongue. She didn't want him to stay for coffee—yes, she did—oh, grief, where was her brain?

Nyall's answer was to toss her a chilly look. Clearly he was not enamoured of her treating him as if he'd just arrived to do a spot of dealing.

'Are you going to come out with me or not?' he questioned bluntly.

Happiness rioted through her. Nyall wanted her to go out with him! She took her gaze from him, finding the top of her desk of interest. Don't be an idiot, warned her head. A few dates, and back to square one, listening for a phone that never rang. She couldn't face going through that again. She raised her glance. 'Not!' she replied.

'Why not?' he fired bluntly.

'Why not?' she queried back, and with a dreadful feeling inside Avena came to earth with a bump as she realised, with Nyall's talk of chemistry, that all he was interested in was making the conquest that had evaded him that night she had dined with him in his apartment.

It hurt. Pain seared through her as she recalled his, 'Oh, Avena, girl. I want you.' Let him think that she had progressed some since that awakening night when 'letting one's hair down' had taken on a new meaning. She had told him of the chemistry he aroused in her, and now he was after that which he seemed to think was his due. And that was as much as she was to him.

Oh, how it hurt. She wanted him gone. Gone so she could lick her wounds in private. She felt desperate, and in her desperation sought for some sure way to make him go.

'I thought I'd made it plain from the beginning, Nyall——' she thought she'd found that way '—that I'm not in line to promote this company via your bedroom.'

Heavens, he didn't like that! It was patently obvious at once that by no means did he take kindly to her remarks. Raw hostility stared back at her as she attempted not to flinch from the sudden swift malevolence in his dark gaze.

'Just what the hell are you suggesting?' he clipped.

'You're the one doing the suggesting, not me,' she hurled back while her nerve lasted. 'I'm merely telling you that there's no way I'm going to bed with you for the sake of Marton Ex . . .'

Oh, help! The murderous look that came to Nyall's face caused her voice to fade. And she only just managed to stifle a scream when, in one moment, he covered the space between them and caught hold of her arms in a fierce grip. She trembled in panic, because from the look on his face he was either going to punch her jaw or kiss her. She feared both, though a punch on the jaw seemed the lesser of the two evils. If he kissed her she'd be lost.

He did not kiss her, nor did he hit her. And she could only guess that, as furious with her as he was, some of her fear and panic must have communicated itself to him, for one moment his fingers were biting into her flesh and the next he was throwing her arms from him. 'I thought you knew me better than that!' he snarled, and the door crashed to after him.

And never had Avena felt more riddled with confusion. Nor had she got herself anywhere near composed when two minutes later Tony charged into her office.

'What have you done to Nyall Lancaster?' he demanded. And, proving he had been hovering, he added, 'He strode past me in a fine rage.'

'We had a fight,' Avena replied tautly, at the end of her rope. 'And if you want to keep your finance director don't say another word!'

Tony opened his mouth, then closed it. And to her surprise, without another word, he went. As he went she became enmeshed once more in the muddle of her emotions.

Yes, she did know Nyall better than to suggest he would attempt to blackmail her into bed by using the company she worked for. For that was what her suggestion had amounted to. Of course she knew him better than that. She trusted him.

For goodness' sake, would she have dined with him at his apartment if she did not trust him? So, OK, they had kissed at his apartment, but as well as tell her 'I want you' he had also left it to her to decide if she wanted to give herself to him. He hadn't pressured her in any way. Neither had she felt in any way threatened. She had walked to the door and he had let her go.

Avena was in the middle of a whole welter of remorse. She had probably so offended Nyall that she'd be lucky if he didn't look through her should she accidentally meet him again and not merely walk by without speaking. Then she remembered his elegant blonde companion at that nightclub, not to mention his glamorous appendage at that art gallery, and suddenly she wasn't feeling anywhere near as remorseful as she had.

She didn't like being in love. It hurt, it confused, and, damn him to hell, she was not going to be picked up and dropped down. And what was more she was going back to giving men a wide berth, going back to being not available. Going back to being the person she had been before she had met Nyall Lancaster. Before him she had deliberately avoided going out with types like Brian because she had found they were more interested in her face than her brain.

She grew confused again. Having grown to know Brian a little, his type didn't seem as bad as she had thought—once certain ground rules had been agreed. And besides, there *was* no going back. She was in love with that damned philanderer, Lancaster.

So all right, she'd been out with a couple of other men too, but there was absolutely nothing she, nor he, for that matter, could do that would kill that love. It was there and, try to drum up hate for him though she might, it would stay there, and there was not a single solitary thing that she could do about it.

Avena tried to immerse herself in her work but could not concentrate, so took herself off for a short walk around. She returned to Marton Exclusives fifteen minutes later and went straight in to see Tony.

'I want a week off,' she told him without preamble. She never took her full holiday entitlement so there was plenty owing to her.

'Take a seat,' he suggested. She only wanted a yes or no; she remained standing. 'You've obviously got a problem,' Tony said after a moment. 'Anything I can help you with?'

Had it not been for his insistence that she go to the Oakby Trading headquarters opening, she wouldn't have had a problem to start with. 'Nothing,' she answered, quite well aware that both her sisters and her mother would have full knowledge of any problem she shared with him by the time she got home. 'I just want a week off, that's all.'

'You sound as if you'd take it anyway, even if I did say no.'

'Try me!'

'Let's hope you come back in a better mood.'

Oh, that it was that easy! Avena returned to her office, realising that, if she was going to take a week off and go down to Kembury that night, she had better find some concentration from somewhere. There were a few loose ends in her work which would have to be tied up before she could take her tidy-minded soul anywhere.

Thinking about loose ends reminded her that she had better ring Brian Goss; she was supposed to be going out with him that night. 'I've decided to go away for a week,' she told him once she had acquainted him with the fact that she was cancelling their date.

'I could probably get some time off too,' he hinted, ever hopeful.

'I'll ring you when I get back,' she told him.

'And if you don't—I'll ring you.' He was good for the ego, was Brian—but he wasn't Nyall.

Avena knew that her decision to get away was the right one when, having worked late, she arrived home to see that the cars of both her sisters were parked on the drive.

She went into the house in no mind to suffer an evening, let alone the succeeding days, listening to a repeat from her sisters, aided by her mother, of Tony's 'What have you done to Nyall Lancaster?', followed by an inquisition into what her fight with him had been about.

'Lovely to see you!' she observed brightly as she stepped briefly into the drawing-room to be the instant focus of attention for three pairs of eyes. 'Though I can't stop; I'm just on my way upstairs to pack.' And, addressing her parent, she added, 'I'm going away for a few days, Mother.'

She was halfway out of the room by the time Lucille, the first to get her breath back, came after her. 'Where are you going?' she wanted to know. And have Gran's phone constantly ringing as they thought up fresh questions? Not likely!

Avena kept on going. 'I haven't decided yet. To the coast most probably; I'll head the car in that direction, anyway.'

She made it to her room without Lucille following her and hurriedly packed a case with the things she thought she would need. Gran wasn't due home for another week, but she had intended to go down and air the cottage for her anyway. Avena knew her grandmother would be only too pleased for her to use her home in her absence.

Before she could leave, however, she once more had to run the gauntlet of the other Alladice women.

'Tony said you had a fight with Nyall Lancaster today.' Lucille did away with tact when Avena came down the stairs with her case and looked to be on her way out before her sister could find out more.

'Oh, yes,' she replied non-committally, and saw Lucille glance to their mother for assistance.

'Do you think that's wise, dear?' Dinah Alladice joined forces with her eldest daughter.

'Wise?'

'Oh, for goodness' sake, Avena!' Coral exclaimed impatiently. 'Nyall Lancaster could do Marton Exclusives extreme harm!'

'Not to mention the extreme good he could do them!' Avena retorted, when she hadn't meant to join the argument at all. 'Sorry, I have to dash—I want to book into a hotel before ten if I can. I'll be home soon,' she told her mother. And to her sisters she added, 'Be as good as you can be.'

She left speedily, hearing a chorus of 'Really!' from the drawing-room, but experienced an overwhelming relief that she had got away with no more of an argument than that.

She was feeling in dull and listless spirits again by the time she reached her grandmother's cottage and went in, realising that she had left in such a hurry that she had forgotten to go and see Mrs Parsons to beg some bread and milk.

Still, the village shop would take care of that and, anyhow, who was hungry? Avena went up to the room that was hers and which overlooked the pretty garden at the back of the cottage. Her grandmother's occasional gardener had been and mown the lawn, she noticed in the failing light and she decided to put in some time on the weeds during the coming days.

She lay down on top of her bed wondering what else she had hoped to achieve by taking a week off work. The fact that she was in love with Nyall, and that he'd run a mile if ever he found that out, would still be there when she got back.

Avena slept fitfully, but when she got up on Saturday she had resolved that she would use this week to sort herself out. It seemed to her then that she was at the crossroads of her life. It was decision time. Without haste she would use her holiday to decide how she wanted to change her life—leave home, leave her job, whatever.

But, since she was going to come to her decisions without haste, and first things came first, she showered, dressed, and, since a classic chignon did not exactly go with jeans and a baggy white shirt, she left her hair loose save for tying it back from her face with a ribbon. Next, she went out to the village store and purchased some groceries.

By midday she had breakfasted, vacuumed and polished and was up in her bedroom cleaning the small window-panes when, lifting the window-catch, it came away in her hand.

It had been loose for a while, she recalled as she went down the stairs for a screwdriver. She returned upstairs to refix the catch, and soon realised why she had never taken it off to do so before. It appeared unfixable; the design was intricate and the wood, as solid as steel, seemed to be impenetrable. What was needed, she very soon realised, was some pure male brute force.

Well, she certainly couldn't go anywhere and leave her grandmother's home unsecured! So where, early on a Saturday afternoon—the chance of a carpenter less than remote—did one find a husky male?

The doorbell sounded. She smiled. Right on cue. Mr Reeves next door might not, at fifty going on sixty, be quite the husky male, but if he'd come bearing a cabbage or rhubarb or produce from his garden, as he was known to do, then since he was more *au fait* with window-catches than she would ever be she was going to invite him in.

Avena tripped lightly down the stairs, a smile on her face as she pulled back the front door—only for her smile promptly to fade.

Her heart thundered. She didn't believe it. She blinked. He was still there. He wasn't holding a cabbage. He wasn't holding a bundle of rhubarb. He wasn't Mr Reeves! Who he was—and she still didn't believe it because he didn't know where her grandmother lived so couldn't be here—was none other than Nyall Lancaster!

CHAPTER SEVEN

SPEECHLESSLY, Avena stared at Nyall. No one knew she was here! She opened her mouth; no sound came. How...? What...? She put a nervous hand to her hair and then became aware that, with her hair loosely tied, dressed in a baggy shirt and with no make-up on, she felt totally defenceless.

Nyall stared stonily back at her. If he had noticed that she was nervous, on the defensive, he gave no sign, but, after long seconds of just standing there looking at her he demanded grimly, 'You're here alone?' And that, his tone, his nerve—for it was quite obvious that he thought she was entertaining some male—brought her away from feeling defenceless.

'And you're too much of a gentleman to intrude on a girl's love-nest!' she erupted.

His jaw jutted aggressively. '*Are you*?' he thundered.

'I don't have to take this!' she snapped, but even as she went to slam the door on him she found that he had acted faster, and was pushing his way in. It was beneath her dignity to scream for help. Then she saw what seeing him had made her forget—that she still had a screwdriver in her hand.

She stepped back. 'Since you are here, you can do me a favour,' she told him sniffily. 'I need a man up-stairs——' She broke off, a blush of colour rushing to her face when, all aggressiveness suddenly and swiftly going from him, she saw Nyall cock a sardonic eyebrow.

'I don't usually like my women so forward,' he remarked. 'But——' his mouth twitched '—anything to oblige.' To her horror she felt her own lips twitch. She didn't want to laugh; she didn't. She wanted to stay mad at him. Oh, Lord, without effort he could make a nonsense of her.

'Here—you'll need this,' she told him soberly, and thrust the screwdriver at him. 'I need a window fixing.'

'After you,' he accepted, and as he came the rest of the way in and closed the door she led the way upstairs.

'There.' Avena pointed as they entered her bedroom. 'The window-catch came off as I was cleaning the windows. I've tried to mend it but the wood's too hard. It's—er—fortunate you came along,' she threw in, fishing madly to find out what the devil he was doing here. Her mother was her best guess as to from whom he had gleaned her possible whereabouts.

Nyall glanced up from examining the window-frame. Pig of a man, he knew exactly what she was asking, but would he answer? Would he hell! 'I just couldn't leave here with the property unsecured.' Ah, that brought forth some response.

'You're going somewhere?' he asked point-blank.

The nerve of it! It was not the slightest business of his! 'Didn't my mother mention that I thought of holidaying on the coast?'

He grinned, and her heart somersaulted. 'She also said that lovable though you are...'

'My mother said I was lovable?' she scoffed.

'Word of honour,' he confirmed, making her wonder what her mother was up to. 'She also said that, lovable though you are, you can be a mite contrary at times.' That sounded more like the mother she knew. 'Your mother felt there was a fair chance you would head this way.'

'So she gave you this address.'

'As you see,' he confirmed.

'And you decided that, this being a lovely summer's day, you'd come and see what this part of the world looked like. Even though I might have been—er—heavily—er—involved with someone?'

'But you aren't,' he replied casually, and frustratingly avoided her unspoken question of why he had come by pronouncing, 'It's not the wood that's too hard—you've got the wrong type of screwdriver.'

'Oh,' she mumbled. She hadn't known that there were different types. They all looked the same to her.

'Presumably your grandmother has a tool-box?' he hinted.

'I'll go and have a look.'

'It'll probably be quicker if I come with you,' he decreed with masculine superiority.

'I bet you can't make a cake!' she sniffed—and, dammit, loved it when his eyes lit up with amusement.

He followed her back down the stairs and, having extracted a box of tools from the cupboard under the stairs, Avena stood by while Nyall sorted through it. She looked at his dark bent head and loved him. Loved him in casual clothes—sports shirt and trousers. Loved the way...

'Ah, found it!' he exclaimed, extracted an implement that didn't look anything like a screwdriver to her mind, and took it, together with an oil-can and a piece of cloth, back with him up to the bedroom.

Avena stood by while Nyall got busy. What did one say in situations like this? Would you like a cup of tea? She didn't think so. Because she so badly wanted him to stay, she wanted him quickly gone. She must not try to prolong his visit by offering him tea. Seeing him so unexpectedly had already made her feel weak, vulnerable. Much better if he went as soon as he'd done the job.

'That'll do it!' Nyall commented, having done a very thorough job and oiled the latch and hinges while he was about it.

'I'll put the things away. The bathroom's next door if you want to wash,' she offered, knowing from experience the impossibility of oiling anything without getting some of it on one's hands.

'Thanks,' he murmured, and went to the next room.

Avena was standing in her bedroom doorway when he emerged on to the small landing. 'I didn't say thank you,' she smiled, aware that she was all churned up because at any moment he would be gone. 'Would you like a cup of tea?' she asked in a rush, and laughed self-consciously as she informed him, 'According to my grandmother, if one wants to keep on the right side of window-latch fixers one should always offer tea.'

Nyall was close, so close that she could see into his eyes. 'Am I allowed to comment that, of late, you've shown remarkably little interest in keeping on the right side of me?' he questioned softly.

'Um...' He was looking at her gently. Her backbone was melting. She strove hard for coherent thought. 'Yes, well, I mean, it's only recently that I've discovered what a whiz you are with window-catches,' she smiled, and felt her heart loop the loop when Nyall raised his right hand and tenderly stroked the back of it down the side of her face.

'Oh, you're so lovely,' he murmured, and Avena was speechless once more.

Her heart pounded and all she could do was to stand there and look at him. She felt too mesmerised to move. But Nyall moved. He bent down, his head coming nearer; she knew he was going to kiss her, and still she could not move.

She felt his kiss to her mouth—the merest whisper of a kiss—and could not take evasive action. Her head told her to resist, but she had been starved of his kisses, and needed their salve to the hurt, the emptiness she had endured.

'D-did I say thank you for the window?' she asked huskily, looking up into that dear face so close to hers. She honestly could not remember if she had thanked him or not.

'May I take another kiss for my reward?' he asked, his tone softly teasing.

Avena reached up and placed her lips against his, and as he gently took her in his arms an inner sigh trembled through her. She wanted to cry his name, but settled for holding on to him as he took the kiss she offered. She held him more tightly, and knew a rush of joy when his arms firmed about her.

Their kiss broke, and not wanting him to go, not yet, she placed her arms around his waist and rested her head against the solid wall of his chest. It was bliss, pure and simple, to stand like that with him, for Nyall seemed in no hurry to go.

She felt the feather-light kiss of his lips to the top of her hair, and raised her head to look at him. 'You're so beautiful!' seemed to be wrenched from him as he gazed down into her face, his eyes taking in its perfect contours, her delicate colouring, the brilliant blue of her eyes.

'I'm—er—not wearing any make-up,' she stated, and felt a touch awkward at such a stupid remark.

But, as he salved her hurt by taking her in his arms, he dissolved any trace of awkwardness she felt by murmuring softly, 'Little love, you don't need any.'

And for that she did what any red-blooded female would have done—she kissed him. She was kissed back and as Nyall's arms tightened yet more about her she wanted more than that one kiss. Her arms tightened about him too, she leaned her body against him, and the next time he kissed her there was an added warmth, an added passion there.

And Avena felt passion stir in her too. The excitement she felt just by being in his arms began to flicker into a fire of wanting. Nyall pressed his body against hers. She moaned softly; she wanted him, loved him and if wanting him was wrong she did not care.

He heard her soft moan and knew it for the sound of desire that it was. His strong arms enveloped her as he traced kisses over her eyes, her nose, her mouth, her throat. 'Sweet love,' he breathed, his endearments wonderful in her ears.

Then he was holding her tightly to him with one arm while he kissed her and caressed her, one hand finding its way beneath her loose shirt. Avena felt the warmth of his touch at the silken skin of her back and as her need for him spiralled with her pleasure so too did she want to feel his skin.

'May I t-touch you?' she asked.

Nyall looked down into her eyes. She had no idea what her eyes were saying but there was a most definite warmth in his. 'I wish you would,' he said softly, and she smiled, and he smiled, and he kissed her and her searching fingers found their way beneath his shirt, and she knew more bliss in feeling his all male, muscled back beneath her seeking hands.

His lips were on hers once more as unhurriedly his hands sought the softer contours of her body. She felt his hands at her breasts and gloried in his touch. She felt yet more joy when with expert fingers he undid her bra, and she gripped him tightly when his caressing hands returned to capture her breast, now naked beneath her shirt.

'Oh, Nyall!' she gasped when he moved his thumbs lightly over the hardened tips he had roused.

'Oh, Avena, love,' he responded, to her utter delight, and said, 'I want to look at you.'

Her breath caught. He meant without her shirt, she knew that. No man had ever seen her uncovered breasts before.

'I—um—want to see you too,' she replied bravely, and reached up and kissed him and kept her lips on his when she felt his exploring fingers at the buttons of her shirt.

Then his arms came around her and tenderly he kissed her, tenderly he broke his kiss and looked down into her face and only when he pulled her close again did she realise that he had somehow taken not only her shirt and bra from her but that he had shed his shirt too.

'Oh!' she gasped as her throbbing swollen breasts came into contact with his naked, hair-roughened chest.

'You object, sweetheart?' he murmured, but she could tell from his tone that he knew she did not.

'I want you,' she said for answer, and held on to him fast while his strong, powerful arms came about her and his hands travelled her skin.

Then he was pulling back again and, after holding her gaze with his for some seconds, slowly he looked down, and a gasp of admiration broke from him. 'Your body is as beautiful as the rest of you,' he breathed, and tenderly kissed first one breast and then the other.

Avena knew that her colour was high. 'Nyall.' She breathed his name, and stroked a tingling hand over his bare chest. He stilled, and she looked up. There seemed to be a question in his expression. Her answer was to lay her mouth gently against his. 'Please,' she whispered, and he looked at her for one second more, then picked her up in his arms and carried her to the bed.

He laid her gently upon it, and leaned down and kissed her tenderly, before bending to the fastenings of her jeans. She swallowed hard when he pulled her jeans from her. Instinctively she put down a hand so that she did not part with her briefs.

Whether Nyall understood her moment of shyness or not she did not know, but he straightened, admiring her considerable length of shapely leg and thigh, and, before discarding his trousers, he joined her on the bed. She closed her eyes.

He had stayed with his brief underwear, she discovered when a moment later he moved close up against her. She felt his body like a second skin next to hers as he kissed her and they pressed towards each other. She heard his groan of wanting, and was thrilled by it. He lay half over her, and she just had to run her fingers over his back.

Nyall took the ribbon from her hair and buried his face in the rich gold of her by then tousled locks. Then he pulled back to stroke her gently, caress her. He whispered kisses down her throat to her breasts and then kissed each one in turn, capturing and moulding with his mouth each hardened pink tip.

Avena was almost screaming out her need for him when she felt his caressing hands at her belly, at her thighs. And she wanted only to assist him when, tenderly, he went to remove her briefs.

She was totally naked when he next pulled away from her. 'Exquisite!' he crooned of her body, of her face and of her cloud of hair, and, starting at her mouth, he traced kisses the length of her body.

'Nyall!' she cried urgently when his tantalising fingers left her rounded buttock. 'I—I need you so badly.'

'Shh,' he soothed, but had his fingers on the last remnant of his own clothing when Avena realised she had something to tell him most urgently.

'Nyall!' she said quickly, and that something different in her tone must have alerted him, because he paused in what he was doing.

'Something worrying you, sweetheart?' he asked considerately.

'Nothing.' She smiled lovingly. 'But—um—in case you thought there has, well, there hasn't.'

He dropped the sweetest of kisses on her mouth. 'May I have a translation?' he enquired.

'Sorry,' she apologised at once, aching with her need for him and wanting it said so that he would enfold her in his arms again and make her his. 'I let you think I'd—um—been with other men—you know, made love with them. But...'

'But you haven't?'

Shyly she smiled up at him. 'I haven't,' she owned, and held out her arms to him. He smiled back, seemed about to kiss her, and then stilled! Suddenly he halted as if frozen. He shook his head as if to clear it. Then, while she was watching, and to her absolute astonishment, not to say disbelief and utter incredulity, as if he had just been shot he abruptly leapt off the bed and, with a speed she could not credit, slammed into his trousers.

'Nyall!' she gasped. Virgin or no, she darn well knew that this wasn't the way it was meant to go. 'What—wh...what are you doing?' she cried, blinking, unable to believe her eyes.

'I need to...' he began, flicked just one glance at her totally naked and beautiful face and body, and, ripping his glance from her, moved and in one stride had collected the remainder of his clothes and—astoundingly—was gone!

Avena was still lying there stunned when she heard a car start up and roar away as if all the devils from hell were after it.

It took an hour before Avena, still expecting him to come back, had calmed down sufficiently to realise that he was not going to. To realise, and to wrestle with the only reason left to her. To do away with the many had hes...had shes...was it thats...had it beens...and finally to accept, to her complete hu-

miliation, that she had offered herself to Nyall
Lancaster as he had intended she should—but purely
so that he could reject her.

She did not want to believe it, but for a man who
had frankly stated within the first few minutes of conversation with her that he wanted her in his bed there
was no other explanation. Without doubt he was an
eye-for-an-eye man. Which made it mortifyingly obvious that as a result of her so deeply offending him
with her remarks about promoting or not promoting
Marton Exclusives through his bed—indeed men-
tioning bed at all in relation to business—Nyall had
decided to make her desperate in her need purely for
the pleasure of dropping her from a great height. He
could not have more clearly told her, No, thanks, not
for any reason, had he engraved it on her soul. And
it *hurt*.

It was no wonder to her, after she had reached these
indelible conclusions, that she felt fidgety, restless and
unable to settle. She felt she wanted to hide herself
away and not come out again for a very long time.
Now, with Nyall knowing where she was, she suddenly felt too exposed.

With only the vaguest notion of what she was about,
Avena began to collect up her belongings. She had
her case packed, milk disposed of, bread in her
grandmother's freezer before she gave serious thought
to where she was going.

She had no intention of returning to her home, that
was certain. Had her mother not told Nyall where he
might find her none of this would have happened,
and she would not now be feeling so emotionally
bruised and battered.

A stray strand of fairness chose that moment to penetrate the utter dejection Avena was feeling. Perhaps it wasn't all down to her mother. Her parent had done no more than make a guess at where she would be and furnish Nyall with the address. She could hardly blame her mother that she had reacted so—wantonly seemed about the only humiliating word to fit—once she had felt Nyall's mouth over her own.

She did blame her mother for that 'lovable' though, and felt that she never wanted to return again to that home where her mother thought her 'lovable'—or so she'd said to Nyall, purely because she wanted him to think so. Avena objected to being 'sold' by her mother. She felt betrayed.

Avena woke up on Sunday in Weston-Super-Mare, the coastal resort she had driven to the day before. It was filled with holiday-makers and she had been lucky to find a hotel room. She was glad it was crowded; what better place to be anonymous and left alone to think one's own thoughts? Though when it came to thoughts she wished that she could get away from those as easily.

Nor was it so easy to be on her own, she discovered, when any unattached, and a few attached, males staying in the hotel seemed to think they were the answer to a maiden's prayer.

'I'm off men at the moment.' She was forced to be blunt to one hopeful who seemed to pounce on her whenever she appeared.

'I could change all that,' he promised.

Oh, God! For the next few days she stayed mainly in her room where disabling thoughts of Nyall haunted her. Thoughts of how she had been with him, how he had been with her, and, worst of all, that rejection. It became a nightmare to her. It took some living with.

On Wednesday she debated about sending her mother a 'having a lovely time' postcard. She decided against it. But on Friday, feeling no more inclined to return home than she had last Saturday, she had surfaced sufficiently from Nyall's rejection of her to recall that she had told her parent she would be away for a few days only.

She knew that her mother always went out to lunch on Friday and at one o'clock she rang home. 'I expect I've missed my mother?' she asked Mrs Parsons.

'I'm afraid you have.'

'Would you tell her that I'm having such a wonderful time that I'll probably go to the office straight from here on Monday?' she requested pleasantly, then chatted for a brief while, and, having salved any prickings of conscience—that didn't know any better—that her parent might conceivably be a tiny bit worried because she hadn't heard from her, ended her call.

Then she realised that she would have to return home on Sunday. Her grandmother was coming back that day, and while it was unthinkable not to be at the airport to meet her, she was hopeful of persuading her grandmother to stay with them overnight rather than just pick up her car and, after her journey, drive on to Kembury.

Then it was that Avena got down at last to think about what she was going to do with her life.

Intending to be away at first light, Avena settled her hotel bill on Saturday evening, and, wondering why, when she should have looked a wreck because of all the sleep she'd lost, she somehow didn't, left Weston-Super-Mare early on Sunday morning and headed her car in the direction of London. Or, to be more precise, the airport.

She had a fair way to drive, but though her thoughts lighted on her grandmother from time to time it was Nyall who was still dominating her thinking.

To get her mind off him she tried to concentrate on how yesterday she had known what she was going to do. First and foremost she was going to cut Nyall Lancaster out of her life as if he had never been. Not that he would be making any efforts to get in touch again. But she never wanted to hear his name again and since her two sisters would not refrain from referring to him whenever they felt like it she was going to leave home.

A bit drastic perhaps, but it seemed to her then that she would probably have come to the decision to find a place of her own soon anyway. The time had come to move out.

And, come tomorrow, she was going to tell Tony and Martin that she was leaving. She would, out of common decency, stay on at Marton Exclusives long enough to see her successor settled, then she would take a look round to see what else was on offer. With luck, the new financial director would be female and pretty—let them take *her* to an Oakby Trading trade evening, she thought sourly, and gave a shaky sigh. Oh, for heaven's sake, when would she stop thinking about him?

Her heart had briefly picked up speed several times during her week in Weston-Super-Mare whenever some man of a similar height and bearing as Nyall had come anywhere into her line of sight. It did it again when, arriving at the airport, she saw another such one. It wasn't him, of course, but over a week had gone by now, and it still wasn't getting any better.

She parked her car and locked it, and was finding her way out of the many-storeyed car park when, to prove that it wasn't only men the height and shape of Nyall that could send her pulses racing, her heart picked up tempo as a long sleek dark car almost identical to Nyall's pulled up beside her.

Avena calmed herself; Nyall was many miles away. But, because the long sleek model was blocking her path, she was obliged to stay put until it had completed whatever manoeuvre its driver intended and moved on.

But the car did not complete its manoeuvre. Oddly, it stayed exactly where it was, blocking her path. She was hemmed in! She was in no particular hurry—her grandmother's plane wasn't scheduled to land yet; she could afford to be patient while the driver sorted himself out.

But he did not sort himself out. Avena was still comparatively calm when she saw the driver's door open. And when a tall, dark-haired man extracted his length from behind the steering-wheel and looked directly at her, so that her heartbeats clamoured, she knew that this was for real! She was not just seeing Nyall in every man of similar build because he meant so much to her. This *was* for real!

He was real! It *was* Nyall—and, from his stern, unsmiling expression as he looked at her, she sensed that he meant business. Her heartbeats did not merely clamour then; they accelerated and positively exploded with speed. She was blocked in, a prisoner, and Nyall was swinging his impressive length athletically over the bonnet of his car, and, as her mouth fell open, he was there standing right there beside her!

Disbelievingly, still trying to make sense of his being there, she gaped at him. And for long, silent, brooding seconds he stared back. But he was the first to speak. 'Avena.' He spoke her name quietly, calmly. 'I—need to talk to you.'

He needed to talk to her! That released her from her frozen immobility. In a flash her mind winged back to those last words she had heard him say. 'I need to...' he had started to say—and had gone, leaving her naked and bewildered. Uncaringly left her stripped both mentally and physically.

And to hear those 'I need to' words again after a week of being rejected, dejected and dead inside... Suddenly Avena came to life, came to furious, rocketing-up-from-despair, raging life.

'Did I forget to make you that cup of tea?' she shrieked, and, her outrage with him too much to contain, she swung a two-handed fist at him in a sideways swipe which, had he not smartly dodged back out of the way, should have dislocated his jaw.

'Steady!' he warned, catching hold of her when from the force of her movement she went off balance.

Steady? She'd kill him! Angrily she pushed him away.

'Who the hell do you think you are that you can do what you did to me and for one isolated moment think that *I* should *ever* want to talk to you?' she spat. My stars, his gall, his unmitigated gall!

'In point of fact I didn't do anything to you,' Nyall replied, calm where she was blowing a fuse, his level look fixed on the veritable fire of fury flashing in her eyes.

'Thanks for making me sound like a trollop!' she snapped, her colour high as she realised that it sounded as if she was complaining because he had *not* made love to her.

'Never in a million years would you be any sort of trollop,' Nyall stated evenly.

She didn't need an argument. 'I've better things to do than "talk" to you!' she told him loftily. 'Kindly move this piece of metal,' she demanded imperiously. 'I want to get by.'

His eyes glinted at her tone, but he was still bent on having a conversation with her, it seemed. For instead of taking her to task as she expected he, to her further astonishment, leaned over and opened the passenger door.

'Get in,' he commanded. 'We can't talk here.'

The *nerve* of the man. 'We can't talk anywhere, full stop, Lancaster. Move this heap so I can go and meet my grandmother.' His answer was to favour her with a steely-eyed determined look.

But her astonishment was overtaken by total disbelieving incredulity when he stated, 'Your mother is here with her car and is already at the arrivals area ready to meet your grandmother.' And, while Avena's eyes went saucer-wide, he declared toughly, 'I've things to say to you that have waited a week to be said—I don't intend to wait any longer!'

Before Avena knew what he was about, he had bundled her into his car and, while she was still getting her breath back, had swiftly vaulted to the driver's side—Olympic standard not in it—was inside, locked in the car with her, and was speeding out of there.

Avena's mouth fell open again, and she had only just grasped on to the fact that for her mother to be here to meet her grandmother, and for Nyall to be here too, must mean that he was in cahoots with her mother, when she grasped something else. She, Avena Alladice, had just been kidnapped!

CHAPTER EIGHT

KIDNAPPED! Avena was still taking that on board when it dawned on her that they had already left the airport. 'Take me back *immediately*,' she demanded.

'Once we've had our...talk, I'll take you anywhere you want to go,' he answered evenly, and she wanted to pound the living daylights out of him. He thought that he could treat her the way he had and that she would want to say another word to him! He could boil in hell!

Mutinously she stared out of the side-window. She had no idea where he thought he was taking her—and she wouldn't ask. She had just spent a most mortifying week in the darkest despair. He thought he could just turn up, snap his fingers, and she would be willing...

She dragged her thoughts away from that word willing. Willing! Confound it, eager, panting for him to take her, practically begging him to make her his wouldn't be overstating it! And he'd dropped her. As if she had been a hot coal he'd dropped her. And he thought he could just stroll up and she'd be avid to hear anything he had to say; he could go and take a running jump.

They had been driving for quite some while when it suddenly penetrated her rebellious thoughts that, for a man whose stated object in kidnapping her was to talk, he was saying very little. Nothing, in fact.

Then Avena started to recognise her surroundings, and experienced a flutter of panic. But that was before she angrily told herself not to be ridiculous. Nyall might be driving them to his home. And he might not be saying anything because he was reserving what he had to say until they got there. But nothing on this earth was going to make her enter his apartment ever again, so he could do his worst.

Quite why she should have panicked at the thought of being incarcerated with him in his apartment she could not understand. It wasn't as if he was likely to throw her on his bed and make mad passionate love to her. Past experience had shown that he had soon grown tired of that—oh, dear heaven, would she never be able to get that out of her mind?

Avena was more determined than ever as Nyall pulled up outside the luxurious building where he had his apartment that he was never going to know the extent of the wounding she had suffered when, just like that, he had walked away from her.

He parked his car in the place reserved for him and turned to look at her. Avena stared unyieldingly straight ahead. Nyall studied her determined-not-to-budge expression for perhaps two seconds longer. Then, with quiet deliberation, he got out of the car and came round to the passenger side.

He opened the door; she ignored him. 'I know that at this moment you're hating me like hell,' he began, 'but——'

'You flatter yourself!' she snorted. 'Hating's too good for you!' But she did hate him that, when she had not meant to utter another peep, he had wrought a response from her.

Nyall bent down; she knew he had. Knew that he was half in the car, looking at her. 'Come with me, please,' he requested politely. She half turned to give him a scathing look and at once wished that she hadn't—there seemed to be something worryingly determined in his eyes.

'You'll forgive me if I decline your so generous offer!' she tossed at him sarcastically, and was staring doggedly straight in front again when she heard him give what sounded like a long-drawn-out breath of unflinching resolution.

'I've said, Avena, that I'd like to talk to you. I should like to do that with some degree of privacy and not out here in the car park.' She shrugged, stubbornly entirely unconcerned with what he wanted. 'I've asked you, nicely, to come with me,' he continued, 'and whatever else is going on in your brain about me you know I won't harm you.' Harm her! He'd damn near crucified her! All this week . . . 'So please, I ask you again, come with me and hear me out and——'

'No!' she cut him off coldly, bluntly, and wished with all her heart that he had not dodged out of the way when, in the last car park, she had attempted to decapitate him.

She did not, however, like the sound of that steadying breath he gave as her 'No!' reached him. And she most definitely did not like the tough-sounding, 'Then, if I have to, I shall carry you,' that followed.

'You wouldn't!' she exclaimed jerkily, slewing round to stare disbelievingly at him. For an answer he reached inside as if to take a firm hold of her. She pushed him away. 'You *rat*!' she becalled him, but moved.

Avena rebelled all the way up to his apartment. The swine! The diabolical, bossy, bigger-than-she-was swine. Oh, for a weapon, something to hit him with!

She had entered his apartment and was standing in the middle of his drawing-room before she wondered at the never-before-known pugilistic person he had aroused in her. She looked at him, and felt weakened suddenly, and wanted that pugilistic person back. Had she been battered and bruised by thoughts of his rejection of her all week merely to find herself—soft in the head—with him once more, and once more back in his apartment? What was she made of, for goodness' sake?

'When are you and my mother getting engaged?' she erupted. She'd soon show him what she was made of. He wanted to talk to her . . . she wouldn't give him chance, whatever it was he felt he wanted to talk to her about.

'Engaged?' Nyall echoed.

'You're obviously in each other's pockets!' she flared.

'Your mother wants what's best for you,' he replied, calm where she was not. 'As,' he added, 'do I.'

'Oh, come on!' Avena flew. 'I know quite well what my mother wants. But you?'

'You've no idea what I want?' Nyall asked, his eyes never leaving her face.

'I know what you don't want!' she exploded.

Nyall stared at her, but she knew he had caught her meaning when, his look steady, his voice steady, he said, 'If you're referring to what happened between us at your grandmother's cottage, then you're wrong.'

'Like blazes I am!' she retorted and realised that, whereas he didn't seem to mind having this conversation, she jolly well did. 'I didn't come here to talk about *that*!' she told him shortly. And although she had determined not to take any part in this whatsoever she found herself asking, in attempting to change the subject, 'So what's so important to talk about that you have to kidnap me, Lancaster?' Oh, grief, he was getting to her. She didn't want him to, but he was. She showed him a belligerent expression.

For long seconds he continued to look at her, then, quite simply, 'I've missed you,' he said, and her stupid, stupid heart began to dance. 'Even while you're looking anti enough to want to stove my head in, I'm glad that you're here.'

Her legs began to feel weak and she felt a desperate need to get some strength from somewhere. 'Look, can you just get on with it?' She adopted a sour note. 'My grandmother's just returned after five weeks away. I would really like to see her before it's six.'

His eyes glinted. 'My God, you've got an acid tongue!' he rapped.

'It's the company I keep!'

He smiled. Unexpectedly, he smiled. And she wanted with everything in her to hate him, but could not. 'Have a seat,' he suggested mildly. It seemed the best idea she had heard in a long while.

'So now I'm sitting comfortably?' she invited from her position on the body-enfolding sofa. But as Nyall pushed an easy-chair opposite so that he could sit near, yet was at an angle to see her every expression, she began to have doubts about the wisdom of taking a seat at all. To get up again, though, might give this clever man a very good hint that she was starting to feel more than a tinge nervous.

'Er—you've been in touch with my mother, obviously.' Those nerves were making her vocal again when she'd had no intention of uttering another word.

'Frequently,' Nyall replied to her surprise.

'Twice,' she catalogued. 'Once to find out that I might be at my grandmother's and,' she went on swiftly, never wanting to refer to that time at her grandmother's again, 'a-and secondly to find out that I'd be at the airport today.' That puzzled her. 'Why?' she asked, wanting to bite her tongue. Since she didn't seem to have any choice she was here to listen to what he had to say, not to ask questions.

'Don't you know?'

'I wouldn't have asked if I did!'

'You've no idea?' She gave him an exasperated look, and went all wobbly inside again when he asked softly, 'How can you be so beautiful and yet so unaware of your charms?'

She was ready to melt—and pulled herself up by her boot-straps. 'If this is a lead-up to showing me your bedroom, forget it. We've done that bit and it didn't work!' He thought she had an acid tongue—she hadn't started yet!

This time, however, Nyall did not seem to mind about her waspishness, and even said, 'I'm hoping you're going to forgive me when I explain——' He broke off—Avena was not ready to let him continue.

'What's to explain?' she questioned snappily. 'I offended you with my remarks about not being prepared to promote the firm I work for through your bed, and you decided to show me that nobody talks like that to you for nothing.'

She tilted her chin and stared at him hostilely, only for some of her hostility to waver when she saw that he was looking back at her in stunned amazement. 'Would you mind telling me what in sweet hell you're talking about?' he asked, recovering quickly.

'You're saying that it wasn't like that? That you didn't deliberately start making—er—love to me so that you could drop me from a great height? Reject me and walk away——?'

'Oh, love,' he cut in, that endearment causing some more of her hostility to fracture. 'You thought that?'

Desperately she tried to get her hostility back. She needed it. She needed its shield. 'All last week I've thought precisely that!' she retorted stonily. But as Nyall left his chair, came to sit beside her on the sofa and reached for her hands she cried in panic, pulling them out of his way, 'Don't touch me!' She was feeling far from the assertive, in-control person she had to be *now*, without the feel of his skin on hers undermining her further.

'All right, all right,' he soothed, withdrawing his hands but staying on the sofa with her just the same. She wasn't too happy about that. Even as he sincerely assured her, 'It wasn't like that,' she was starting to feel extremely anxious about him being so near.

'Wasn't it?' Her belligerence was out again in full force.

'It was not.'

She didn't believe him. Odd that she should trust him yet not believe him. 'So how was it?' she invited, and at once regretted it. 'Forget it.' She countermanded the invitation. Nyall had something he wanted to talk to her about—she was positive it wasn't about *that*! 'So what sort of a week did you have?' she changed the subject sourly.

'One hell of a week!' he replied feelingly. Good; she could not be more pleased to hear it.

'Business that bad, eh?'

Nyall studied her for a moment. 'Even nervous you're a cheeky bitch,' he murmured, but before she could deny the 'nervous' or take exception to the 'cheeky bitch' he was going on. 'My week had little to do with business.'

Great—while she'd been in Weston-Super-Mare breaking her heart over the swine, he'd been living it up on holiday somewhere.

'Not for you Brighton!' she sniffed tartly.

'If last week was a holiday then I never want another one!' he flipped back at her, and practically floored her when he went on to state, 'I spent most of the week going back and forth to Kembury on the off chance that you might have returned.'

'You went back to Kembury?' she asked, her eyes widening.

'I've practically camped out on your grandmother's doorstep,' he confirmed, and while Avena tried to make her brain function so that she might have some clue as to why he would have kept going back to the Worcestershire village Nyall further astonished her by adding, 'When I wasn't physically in Kembury I was dialling your grandmother's number in the hope that you might be there to pick up the phone. And, in between whiles, I was in contact with your mother—she didn't know where you were either.'

'Grief!' she gasped, and, brilliance failing her, 'I had the key to the safe?'

'You had the key to...?' Nyall didn't finish, but said instead, 'We didn't know where you were. And then, on Friday, you rang and left a message with your housekeeper.'

'You knew about that?'

'I rang your mother daily for news of you,' he owned, and while Avena stared at him thunderstruck he revealed, 'She said that you'd definitely be at your desk on Monday, but that, because you were having such a wonderful time——' why he should suddenly look accusing she had no idea; she knew that it had been a lie and that she hadn't had a wonderful time, but he didn't '——you would probably go straight to your office on Monday.'

'Is there anything you don't know?' she exclaimed.

'There's a great deal I don't know,' he answered, 'but which I'm quite urgently hoping to find out!'

'Oh,' she murmured, her brain a poor thing and just not up to coping with this—of sitting through what he was saying and making sense of it when her nerves were jumping and she didn't want to be there but didn't want to be anywhere else either. Why? Why? Why? 'Um—this sounds—serious,' was the best she could come up with.

'It is,' he agreed. 'Which is why, your mother appreciating how urgent it was that I see you——' oh, heavens, if Nyall had phoned daily Avena suddenly realised that she'd be hearing his name from her mother morning, noon and night now! Then she remembered her intention to move out '—as soon as she realised it was today that your grandmother was due back, she phoned to tell me that, from what she knew of you, come hell or high water you'd be at the airport today to meet her.'

Avena stared at him, her powers of comprehension seeming to be asleep. She decided to take it very carefully. 'So...you arranged with my mother that she should meet Gran because——' She broke off to swallow. 'Because you wanted—urgently—to—um—have a—chat—with me.'

Nyall rested his eyes on her; she hoped she looked calmer than she felt. Inside she was a mass of jumping nerves. She wanted to hate him, felt that to hate him might help her cope with the suddenly totally vulnerable person she felt now that her hostility towards him had gone.

But she could not hate him, and felt more totally vulnerable than ever when, his look all of a sudden gentle, he stated quietly, 'I need, urgently, to have a serious chat with you, my dear.'

Her throat dried. 'What—about?' she croaked—and moved back a few inches when it seemed as if Nyall would attempt to take hold of her hands again.

He halted, scrutinising her face, but did not touch her. 'So much, yet basically there are just a few questions I need an answer to.'

He wanted answers from her. Her eyes were large in her face as she looked at him. They didn't come smarter than him in business, so she could rule out that he wanted to tap her brilliant brain for some information. Personal, then? 'You want me to...be your mistress?' she questioned shakily, unable to think of anything else.

'Oh, that it were so simple,' he replied, and suddenly she was angry again.

Grief, what was she that he could wipe the floor with her? 'Forgive me, I forgot,' she snapped, getting rapidly to her feet. 'We've already played that game where I'm all yours—only to find you're not interested!' She moved fast, rocketing across the room afraid that the sudden tears that stung her eyes might show.

She was over at the outer door when Nyall caught her. She felt his hands on her shoulders, and fought him furiously so she could be free.

'I'm going!' she yelled.

'Not yet, you're not!'

She tried a kick to his shin and found that her back was against the door, that she was pinned to it. Nyall had a hand either side of her head while he used his body to keep her prisoner. 'Get away from me!' she spat, the feel of him against her treacherous body weakening her fury.

'You took a swing at me at the airport—you'll have to learn to control that magnificent temper,' he grunted, keeping her there by the force of his body. 'Are you going to behave?'

'Behave? She'd show him behave! She'd show him control! She had one hand free. She bunched it into a fist and punched him in the stomach. His stomach was hard. 'You hurt my hand!' she raged.

'Blame me,' he invited, and she wanted to weep. He was to blame, and *she* was hurting, not just her hand.

'I want to go,' she whispered, defeated.

Gently, Nyall looked down at her. Then, tenderly, he kissed her unhappy face. 'I love you,' he said softly—just like that—and she collapsed forward against him.

'Do you ... tell lies?' she asked, shaken to the core but already not crediting that she had heard him say what she thought he had said.

Nyall gathered her to him and for long, long moments held her against him. 'I may have lied to myself in the past, but anything I say to you from now on will be nothing but the truth.' She could not speak; she could barely stand. 'Are you going to hear me out?' he asked. She still could not speak. 'Do you still want to go?'

She shook her head, and felt his hand beneath her chin as he tilted up her head so that he could see her face. Solemnly, still not believing, she stared at him. Solemnly, he stared at her too.

'Come on,' he urged and, with an arm still about her, he escorted her back to the sofa.

Avena started to feel stronger once she had the solidity of the sofa beneath her. But Nyall's arm was still about her and if this was some new form of punishment for her remarks about bed and business—and she was having the most tremendous difficulty in grappling with the astonishing fact that Nyall had actually said 'I love you', if in fact he had actually said it at all—then she needed that arm away from her. If she was to gather together any of her disjointed wits then, while she wanted him to love her so much that there was no way she could walk out of there until she had heard more, she did not need his weakening, brain-scattering touch.

She pulled away from his hold, wished she hadn't when he let her go, but did feel that small degree stronger and a shade less shaky. Enough to be able to find her voice, anyhow. 'You said something about explaining,' she commented, with only the vaguest notion just then of what he had said he wanted to explain about.

Nyall, though, had instant recall of what they had been talking about, she discovered, when, with a fast-beating heart, she looked at him. 'I've a lot of explaining to do,' he replied gently. 'And not just about why, when you were so utterly adorable in my arms eight long, wearying, agonising days ago, I had to force myself to leave you because I so desperately discovered I needed to think.'

'You needed to *think*!' she echoed, his 'I need to...' indelibly printed on her brain. 'What did you need to think about?' She could no more refrain from asking than fly.

'You, you—and you,' he answered with a self-deprecating smile. 'I should have known when I saw you just three months ago that my world was about to change—but, of course, I didn't.'

'I—er—I'm trying to understand,' she mumbled, the seriousness of her expression perhaps giving away that she felt herself to be on dreadfully insecure ground. 'I—um—think it might help if you didn't talk in riddles.'

'Forgive me,' he answered gently, but owned, 'I'm new to all this.'

Avena was in no way sure what 'all this' was, but, since the man she cared so much about just might have said those words 'I love you', she was going to do her darnedest to stay there and try to take everything in, to hope, to... Oh, could he really have said 'I love you'? She just did not dare ask. For a little while longer she wanted to believe what she thought she had heard. Life would be too bleak after if...

'Er—you said something about when we met,' she abruptly banished her thoughts to prompt.

'It began before we met,' he smiled. 'Oakby Trading was celebrating the opening of its new headquarters when I dropped by to offer my congratulations. I saw you as soon as I entered the room—you were laughing at something that one of the men you were with had said.'

'Walter,' she supplied, her nerves not settling at all as she had hoped.

'It's always some man,' Nyall remarked, and when she looked at him enquiringly he explained, 'That's been a large part of the trouble,' which in no way explained anything to her. 'Most times I've seen you you've invariably been surrounded by a group of admiring males.'

'You're serious?' she queried, not believing it for a moment.

'Look in the mirror some time,' he suggested softly, and went on. 'There you were that first time I saw you, stunningly beautiful, and, while I admit that I've known quite a few beautiful women, I couldn't remember ever before feeling that same surge of excitement that hit me when I looked at you.'

Her mouth fell open. She closed it. 'No!' she denied on a whisper.

'Oh, yes,' he contradicted. 'I found out who you were, who you were with and, I confess, as insurance in case the financial director of Marton's was deadly dull, I suggested I should like to meet you *and* the Marton Exclusives team.'

'Just like that?'

'Just like that,' he agreed. 'Only you, my dear Avena, showed me exactly what you thought of my arrogance by thumbing your nose at me and leaving.'

'You didn't believe "unwell"?'

'Not for a moment.'

She smiled, though how she could when her insides were such a jangled mass of tension and emotion she had no idea. 'I—um—felt you were a man to avoid,' she admitted, but at his alert look nerves bit again, and she went on hurriedly, 'Also, I hold strong objections about using any of the—er—attributes I may have to further the firm's business——'

'I know that,' he interrupted softly. 'Just as I knew within a minute of speaking with you at our next meeting that there was nothing remotely dull about this financial director.'

Avena remembered that meeting, oh, so well. He had not shirked from telling her openly that he wanted her in his bed... Hurriedly she switched her mind away from such memories. 'Had you not happened to drop in at Oakby's trade evening that night, we might never have spoken to each other at all,' she commented quickly to get her mind off the subject.

'And if you believe that you'll believe anything,' he replied.

'You'd have phoned me at the office?' she enquired, startled.

'I did phone you at the office. But first I made sure that you in particular, along with your directors, had an invitation to that trade evening.'

'But,' she gasped, 'I'm sure I remember you being surprised to see me there!'

'You remember me *seeming* to be surprised to see you there.'

'But you knew I would attend?'

'I knew your directors were anxious to do business. I hoped you'd be there.'

'You—um—wanted to see me?'

'I'd seen you once—I couldn't get the picture of you, thoughts of you, out of my head.'

Her jaw dropped in disbelief. 'Honestly?' she asked chokily.

'Believe me,' Nyall answered quietly. 'I want to be more open with you than I've ever been with anyone in my life.'

Oh, how wonderful that sounded. And she wanted to believe it. Just as she wanted to believe that she had heard him correctly when she thought he had said 'I love you'. But she had just been through the most dejected, tormented eight days and just as Nyall had wanted insurance against her being a deadly dull financial director she needed insurance to protect her from plummeting to yet further depths if she had got it all wrong.

'So you saw me,' she documented carefully, 'a week later met me, and a week after that you decided to ring me at my office.'

'And didn't like it one bit when you declined my offer in favour of some lucky devil called James.' Could she believe it—did Nyall sound just the tiniest bit jealous? 'But, to make me feel a whole lot better, later that evening I learned that you were dumping James...'

'You found out differently when——'

'I found out a whole lot of things that night, sweet love,' Nyall cut back in, and while her heart thundered at his endearment he went on gently, 'I arrived at your home to hear you being got at from all sides. Only then did I begin to realise the extent of the pressure you were under, how sensitive you were and— a new one for me—I had an almost overwhelming urge to hold you quietly in my arms until you felt better.'

Oh, heavens, her backbone was as water. 'You— er—instead of holding me you made me laugh.'

'And we had a splendid evening at your village hall. Later you fed me and, while I knew full well that you hadn't planned for me to enjoy any of it, I truly felt I had missed out on a lot by not knowing you sooner.'

'Really?' she questioned, staring at him with huge eyes.

'Only the truth,' he promised. 'I know I quite desperately wanted to kiss you, yet at the same time I felt mixed up, as if it wouldn't be right. I thought it best I should leave.'

Avena remembered that evening as if it had been yesterday. The atmosphere had been electric. 'You did kiss me, though. On the drive, before you went.'

'And remembered your sweet lips in the week that followed when time and time again I wanted to phone you.'

'But didn't.'

'But didn't, because some sixth sense was warning me that I was likely to get my fingers burned. When I did give in and ring, though, what did I get for my trouble but your housekeeper telling me you'd gone away for the weekend.'

'You expected me to wait in for your call?' she smiled.

'I didn't expect to feel furious at the idea that wouldn't leave me that you had gone away with some man. Nor did I expect to feel positively outraged when I was able to speak with you and you intimated you'd given yourself to your partner of the weekend. I stayed much the same way,' he confessed, 'until I received your painting of a purple hyacinth—and your apology revealing how innocent your weekend had been.'

'You sent me a card back,' she recalled dreamily.

'And rang you and, for my sins, invited you to a party.'

'For your sins?'

'There was I, becoming more and more fascinated by you,' he began to explain, again making her heart race, 'and there were you, surrounded by men and totally oblivious of me.'

Oblivious of him? Never. 'From what I recall, you seemed pretty oblivious yourself. You didn't seem in any rush to leave the brunette, or the blonde, either.'

'You're jealous!' he pounced, and looked delighted.

'I didn't say that,' she denied, and saw his pleased look fade.

'Oh, that you had,' he murmured feelingly, and as she looked at him Avena realised, with a start of shock, that Nyall seemed to be quite desperate to have some sign from her that she cared for him.

She was not sure, though, that she felt confident enough to commit herself fully. Yet at the same time she loved him so much that she just had to bend a little. 'Well,' she began shakily, 'perhaps I was a bit—a little bit—jealous.'

He smiled; his smile became a grin. And then, as if he just could not help it, he leaned towards her, took her hands in his and, gently, still holding her hands firm in his, kissed her.

'Oh, I've missed you so,' he breathed on a ragged breath.

'You—have?'

'So much—so many times.'

'I don't think I'm understanding again.'

'Don't you, love?' he asked softly, his eyes on her so loving that Avena began to tremble, and began to believe that maybe she had not been mistaken. Maybe Nyall had said 'I love you'.

'You've ... missed me, you said,' she managed on a gulp of breath.

'I've missed you,' he agreed. 'Yet apart from this past week, when I've been going slowly demented and started to think I might never see you again, I have, at other times, deliberately held back from contacting you.'

Avena well remembered how a week at a time would pass without him contacting her. Two and a half weeks recently, she recalled without effort. And, although an hour ago wild horses would not have dragged the question from her, her trust in what he had said had begun to deepen, and she asked, 'Why? What did I do?'

'You, my darling?' He smiled. 'Nothing but have a sweetness, a charm, and ... to have been born so utterly beautiful.'

She was thrilled, mystified, and in a fog again. 'Well, we all have our faults,' she managed chokily.

'The fault is all mine,' he said softly. 'Mine in that, when I saw how every man you came into contact with drooled over you, I decided that I most certainly was not going to become one of the crowd.'

Avena stared at him, disbelieving, as she tried to comprehend what he was saying. He was exaggerating, of course, about every man she came into contact with drooling over her. However, on recalling how he had stood out from the rest that first time she had seen him, she could never see him as being one of a crowd.

'You're saying that you deliberately didn't contact me when you wanted to?'

'It wasn't easy. Believe me, it wasn't easy,' he assured her. 'I resisted. Oh, how I resisted. Seven days would pass before I gave in to the constant pressure of what I wanted to do. Almost a fortnight passed once before I gave in and took up Spicer's personal invitation to Marton's open day.'

'Tony contacted you personally?'

'I told him I couldn't make it—and then discovered I couldn't keep away. I tried—my God, how I tried. After that Saturday when we had dinner at my place I had to acknowledge that you were really getting to me. I just knew I mustn't get in touch with you again. Yet you were in my head the whole time.

'I dated a couple of other women—nothing heavy,' he inserted, 'but purely in an endeavour to get you out of my head. Only to discover you were daring to date other men when, having seen you everywhere I turned, I found it was not my imagination conjuring you up in my desperation to see you. But...how dared you? You were actually dating other men.'

'I—er—got tired of waiting for you to ring. Angry that——' She broke off. What had she said? Had she revealed too much? She started to panic, and then saw from the tense yet adoring look on Nyall's face that she had no need in the world to panic.

'You were waiting for me to ring? Wanting me to ring?' he asked.

'And furious with you when you did,' she admitted.

'All of which means?' He seemed quite desperate to know and now, Avena knew, was not the time to hold back. But suddenly she was in the grip of shyness, and could not answer him. Nyall, seeming to be yet more desperate, gave the hands he was holding a little shake. 'Please,' he urged. 'You've always been so honest with me.' She swallowed hard, and strain started to fracture his control. 'You're so fair of face—can you not now be honest of heart?' he pressed.

'Honest of heart? Oh, Nyall,' she cried, and could not hold back from telling him, 'I—do—care for you.'

'Love me?' he demanded.

'That too,' she murmured on a shy laugh.

'Sweetheart!' he cried exultantly.

Merely to hold her hands was not good enough then. In the next moment Nyall had hauled her into his arms, close up against his heart, and was crooning words of endearment in her ears.

'Little love, when did you know?' He pulled back to look in her face.

'That Friday. The Friday of our open day. You came up behind me—I didn't know you were even there—and—er—said something about me knowing how to kiss, and I turned round and saw you—and knew.'

'My love.' She was close up against his heart again. Then Nyall drew back and after long moments of just feasting his eyes on her he kissed her. And it was wonderful as, willingly, her lips met his. 'I need...to know more,' he gently demanded as he let some daylight in between them.

It seemed incredible to her that he should want yet more reassurance that she loved him. Though perhaps it wasn't so incredible, she realised, because even though her belief that he loved her was growing and growing she found she still had to ask, 'You did mean it—about being...about loving me?'

'I love you,' he replied without a moment's hesitation. 'Avena, my own, I'm in love with you. So much in love with you that, of late, there have been times when I've begun to doubt my sanity.'

'Oh, darling!' she cried shyly, and was tenderly kissed for that 'darling' before she could begin to tell him what he wanted to know, before she could give him that reassurance he wanted. 'I think the balance of my mind must have taken a little tilt from the first time I saw you,' she admitted.

'Don't, whatever you do, leave it there,' he insisted, and she laughed.

'My normally sane thinking seemed to desert me,' she owned. 'I clearly remember being confused and unsettled—and that was before we'd ever spoken with each other. Then we did meet and went to the village concert and, although of course I wasn't going to admit it, I wasn't too happy when a week went by and you didn't phone.'

'It goes without saying that you weren't used to such treatment,' Nyall stated. 'Trust me to give in the weekend you decide to pay your grandmother a visit.'

'We went out together the next Saturday,' she smiled.

'To that damned party,' he took up ruefully. 'We kissed on the way home, and I was quite desperate to kiss you again at your door—just a kiss on parting. But my control was shaky, not to say shot—and I was afraid to touch you.'

'Honestly?'

'Honestly,' he smiled. 'I must have been crazy to take you anywhere near predators like Goss.'

'Oh, Brian's all right,' Avena assured him, and saw that Nyall didn't care for her defending the man. 'Well, he was when I told him, as you reminded me, that some girls don't,' she laughed.

'He tried?' Nyall seemed outraged.

'So did you,' she thought to remind him.

'That's different!' he stated. 'I should have thumped him when I had the chance. That's what I wanted to do when I entered that nightclub and, like the magnet you are for me, you drew my eyes to you straight away.'

'I didn't think you'd seen me.'

'I spotted you at once, pretended I hadn't as I coped with a riot of emotions because you were out with another man—though God knows what else I thought a woman with all you've got going for you was going to do on a Saturday night—and was off my chair following you the moment I saw you leave your seat.'

'That meeting in the lobby—it wasn't accidental?' she exclaimed.

'I came after you without even thinking—just knew that I had to spend a few moments with you.'

'You didn't—um—seem very pleased to see me.'

Nyall smiled a dry smile. 'I was feeling a fool. It wasn't the way it was supposed to go. You were getting to me, I knew that. But rather than be one of the herd I'd cut you out of my life, hadn't seen you for two weeks—but kept thinking about you.'

'You did?'

'Oh, you heart-breaker, I did. Naturally, in my superior wisdom I told myself it would get easier—only it didn't.'

'Oh!' she sighed blissfully.

'And when I saw you leaving that nightclub with Goss's arm familiarly about you I underwent some very strong murderous emotions. Nor was I too thrilled when, devil take it, the next time I saw you

you were with some earnest-looking type built like a nuclear fall-out shelter.'

'Fergus is my friend Kate's ex-husband. He's taken the divorce pretty badly. I let him bend my ear from time to time.' Avena answered the question she read in Nyall's eyes, but added, 'You went by without speaking.'

'You weren't saying very much either, Miss Nose-in-the-air,' he reminded her.

'What should I have said?' she queried, confessing, to his delight, 'I was pea-green with jealousy. You weren't alone, as I recall.'

'Oh, sweetheart, come here,' he soothed, and sent away all her hurt by holding her fast in his arms, and kissing her oh, so tenderly. When at last he broke his kiss he pulled back to look deeply into her lovely blue eyes. 'How could I ever have imagined that I could best this wealth of feeling I have for you, my dear one?' he breathed. 'These feelings that have kept me sleepless . . .'

'You too?' she sighed.

'You?' She nodded; he hugged her. 'Oh, how well I remember; it was one Friday—the Friday I'd dropped in to Marton's open day. You and I had lunch together, and I was so enchanted by you that I stayed home that evening thinking about you, wanting to phone you, but holding back. For my pains you came between me and my sleep that night. I was awake early with you still in my head. To hell with it, I thought, and, regardless of the hour, rang you anyway.'

'It was eight o'clock,' she informed him, without having to think about it. 'I'd had a pretty fractured night too,' she confessed.

'Thinking about me, I hope,' he grinned. But he was serious as he went on to explain, 'I invited you to have dinner here purely because I wanted to prove that my self-control was as good as ever it had been.'

'And it was,' she filled in. 'We—er—and you let me go.'

'You make it sound easy!' he exclaimed warmly. 'There you were, your wonderful hair down about your shoulders—I wondered at the wisdom of what I was doing the moment you answered the door to me. Yet I couldn't resist, even though all the way here I had tried to instil in myself the necessity of keeping a cool head. But after dinner, when Stuart had dragged himself away from you, you kissed me, and I knew I was in big trouble.'

'But for my having to take my grandmother to the airport early that next morning, we both might have been in very big trouble,' she laughed, saw Nyall realise what she was saying, and was soundly kissed.

'Dear love, I've wasted so much time,' he breathed. 'Though I have to admit that, although I think I'm pretty smart,' he went on with a wry look, 'I wasn't as quick as you to allow what had been staring me in the face for so long now.'

'I'm loving this,' she said, urging him on.

'And I adore your honesty.' He smiled, a warm special smile for her. 'Oh, that I could have been so honest with myself.'

'You haven't been?'

He shook his head. 'It was a week ago last Wednesday when I knew—acknowledged—that I was going to have to do something about you. Thoughts of you were driving me out of my head. I just couldn't get you off my mind.

'So, all right, I'd denied myself the joy of seeing you because every other man seemed to be chasing you, but, I thought, perhaps if I did give in... Forgive me, darling, but I had some vague notion that if I did bed you then perhaps I'd be able to get you out of my head.

'So I rang; later that evening I just caved in and rang—and then discovered, for my sauce, that you just weren't interested. That you were entertaining some man...'

'Er—I lied,' she owned up.

'You what? You wretched woman,' he becalled her lovingly. 'So having made me furious for daring to think you were sitting by the phone waiting on the off chance that I'd call——'

'You seem to know me very well.'

'I know your pride—and I intend to know you much better,' he promised. 'I slammed the phone down in a fine jealous rage at your intimation that you were no longer a virgin. I couldn't sleep. But neither, in my saner moments, could I believe, from what I knew of you, that you'd given yourself to a man like Goss. Nor——'

'Actually, Brian's quite nice when you get to know him,' she inserted prettily.

'I *don't* wish to know that!'

'Sorry,' she laughed, and then realised that she wouldn't feel too kindly if Nyall tried explaining to her how nice the brunette or the blonde was. 'But nowhere near as nice as you,' she attempted.

'Hussy!'

'Go on,' she smiled.

'So there was I, going quietly insane about you, when a couple of days later—with work enough on my desk to keep me busy until midnight—I told my PA I was going out, and came looking for you.'

'Friday,' she documented, and, with a start, exclaimed, 'You came to my office! You said you were passing!'

'Er—I lied,' *he* owned up.

'Oh, Nyall, I do so love you.'

He kissed her. Lingeringly he kissed her. 'You weren't showing your love then,' he murmured.

'We rowed.'

'You provoked me. When you well knew that what was between us was between *us* you had the nerve to bring the company into it. Your comments were unworthy. Even though I wasn't acknowledging exactly what it was that was between us, I knew what we had was worth more than that sort of remark. So where did you get off saying——?'

'Nyall, I'm so sorry,' she rushed in. 'I was hurt, panicking, wanting you gone so that I could cope with the hurt that I was nothing more to you...than a conquest.'

Gently, tenderly, Nyall gathered her to him. 'Never just that,' he breathed. 'Would it help if I told you that no woman has ever aroused in me so many different emotional and highly aware feelings as you?'

'Oh, yes,' she beamed, and was kissed.

'Yet I still wasn't seeing what was in front of my face.'

'You didn't know then that you loved me?'

'It was there, staring at me, but in my determination not to be one of the pack I was at my stubborn worst. What I did know, though, was that after another sleepless night I couldn't rest, and had to see you.'

'You called at my home, and saw my mother.'

'After the way our last telephone conversation ended, I thought it might be an idea to call on you personally. Blow number one was that you weren't there. Blow number two was that you had gone away, and I was consumed with jealousy. Who with?'

'When your mother reminded me that your grandmother was still away and suggested that there was an outside chance you might have gone there, even though I suspected that there was every chance my presence would be most unwelcome, I still had to speed down to Kembury.'

With sensitive fingers, his hands went to her hair. 'Do you mind?' he asked as he began taking out pins and releasing shiny golden strands of her hair from the confines of its chignon.

'Not at all,' she murmured, such love for him welling up in her as her hair fell down about her shoulders.

'You opened the door and, as always, looked absolutely adorable. Can you wonder that, having discovered you were there on your own, I should hardly know why I was there? All I knew, as I avoided all hints from you to know what I was doing at your grandmother's, was that it felt so good to be with you.'

'Oh, Nyall,' she sighed mistily. 'You mended the window-catch,' she added dreamily.

'And took my reward for doing so in a kiss.'

'Ah, yes,' she said.

'"Ah, yes", it was,' Nyall took up. 'There we were, all barriers down, my heart pounding, my control all but gone in my urgent desire for you. Then, as I looked down at you, lying there, trusting, looking at me, trusting, you confirmed that you hadn't been with anyone else, and suddenly it wasn't only my heart that was pounding—my head was pounding too. Did I want to take that trust for a few weeks, months perhaps? And a split-second later, while at the same time I wanted you so desperately, I was asking, Is this what I want, not for me but for *you*? But you wanted me too; I just couldn't think straight.'

'So you—went away.'

'I had to—don't you see? If I hadn't gone then, and quickly, that last remaining thread of control would have snapped. I left you . . . drowning in the confusion of my thoughts and emotions.'

'But . . . you were later able to think?'

'Much later,' he agreed. 'All the way back here I wanted to turn about and come back to you. But I was striving to think clearly—and I promise you that wasn't easy. I knew I mustn't do that, mustn't come back—not until I'd come up with some answers. Answers to why and how what had started out as me wanting you in my bed had been turned completely on its head in that, when you were willing, I was not.'

'It—um—shook you.'

'Devastated me. And then I wasn't even having to think. Like a bolt from the blue, I knew. Suddenly, just like that. With heart-stopping clarity I just knew, without having to analyse the whys and wherefores, that I loved you, that you were a part of me.'

'Oh, Nyall,' she whispered, and just had to reach up and kiss him. He caught hold of one of her hands and placed a caress of a kiss in its palm. 'Did you think then that I might love you?' she asked softly.

'At that stage I was stunned and joyous—and fearful as I went back over everything that had taken place between us. Had I detected a flicker of jealousy that evening at the nightclub when you'd commented "I see you're keeping your hand in"?'

'Yes, you did,' she confirmed.

He kissed the top of her hair. 'I had so little to go on, but over and above everything else I remembered how you'd told me that first time we spoke that you couldn't go to bed with anyone you didn't love. I hung on to that memory when all last week I went demented trying to find you. Then something dreadful struck me, and I knew I couldn't wait until nine o'clock on Monday to be at Marton Exclusives when you arrived.'

'You'd have been at Marton's tomorrow?'

'Way before nine in case you came early,' he confirmed.

'Oh, darling!' she cried, but then recalled something else he had said. 'You said that something dreadful struck you——'

She broke off as a most serious expression came to his face. And suddenly her heart was drumming in anxiety.

'I've been in emotional hell all week,' Nyall began. 'But the emotional turmoil I went through before I realised that I loved you seemed the lesser part of the emotional battering I've taken—and am still taking— at the realisation that followed.'

'Oh?' she queried, the seriousness of his expression affecting her, making her wary, making her fear the worst. 'What . . . realisation was that?' she asked nervously, and, observing her apprehension, he held her more firmly to him.

'Dear Avena, what followed, and followed before I'd barely realised the depth of my feeling for you,

was the concrete knowledge that was suddenly there—
that the reason I had not made you mine was that I
didn't want to take you to my bed for just a few
weeks—or a few months—that I wanted you for
longer than that. That my feelings for you, my love,
are bigger than that. And that it wasn't purely bed
that I wanted. I, sweet love, want you for life.'

A gasp escaped her. 'You . . . d-do?' she asked
chokily.

'I do,' he affirmed. 'I know it now, and I knew it
then. But then I remembered and another dreadful
realisation hit me.'

'Yes?' she urged; oddly, when her heart was beating
ten to the dozen, he seemed to be the more nervous
of the two of them. 'Please tell me, Nyall.'

'That you, keeper of my heart, would not marry
anyone with money—you had said so.'

'Nyall!' she gasped. Was he asking her to marry
him? Dared she believe it? Her heart was not merely
racing, it was thundering along. 'Did I say that?' she
asked, incapable at that moment of having a clue
about what she had said on the subject.

'Didn't you mean it?' he pressed urgently.

Avena swallowed and still couldn't remember, but
she was aware enough of not wanting to marry for
the same reasons as her mother and her sisters. 'I
honestly can't remember what I said, but what I know
for sure is that I would never marry any man *for*
money.'

In that instant his expression cleared. 'Then, since
you tell me that you love me, will you, Avena, my
heart, my love, my dear, dear child of a Monday, will
you marry me for love?'

Avena felt her heart would burst. She had known him for three months and, she realised, for a lot of the time during those months what fair-of-face looks she possessed had been instrumental in keeping her and Nyall apart. She wanted to be apart from him no more.

'Will you?' he urged hoarsely.

She did not keep him waiting any longer. 'Oh, yes, whenever you say,' she accepted warmly.

* * * * *

Tuesday's child is full of grace ...
Look out next month for Eva Rutland's
Private Dancer, the latest book in
our exciting series.

BRIDE'S BAY RESORT

UNLOCK THE DOOR TO GREAT ROMANCE
AT BRIDE'S BAY RESORT

Join Harlequin's new across-the-lines series, set in an exclusive hotel on an island off the coast of South Carolina.

Seven of your favorite authors will bring you exciting stories about fascinating heroes and heroines discovering love at Bride's Bay Resort.

Look for these fabulous stories coming to a store near you beginning in January 1996.

Harlequin American Romance #613 in January
Matchmaking Baby by Cathy Gillen Thacker

Harlequin Presents #1794 in February
Indiscretions by Robyn Donald

Harlequin Intrigue #362 in March
Love and Lies by Dawn Stewardson

Harlequin Romance #3404 in April
Make Believe Engagement by Day Leclaire

Harlequin Temptation #588 in May
Stranger in the Night by Roseanne Williams

Harlequin Superromance #695 in June
Married to a Stranger by Connie Bennett

Harlequin Historicals #324 in July
Dulcie's Gift by Ruth Langan

Visit Bride's Bay Resort each month wherever Harlequin books are sold.

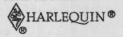

HARLEQUIN ®

BBAYG

You're About to Become a

Privileged Woman

Reap the rewards of fabulous free gifts and benefits with proofs-of-purchase from Harlequin and Silhouette books

Pages & Privileges™

It's our way of thanking you for buying our books at your favorite retail stores.

✂

PROOF OF PURCHASE

HR-PP134

Offer expires October 31, 1996

**Harlequin and Silhouette—
the most privileged readers in the world!**

For more information about Harlequin and Silhouette's PAGES & PRIVILEGES program call the Pages & Privileges Benefits Desk: 1-503-794-2499

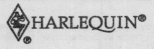

HARLEQUIN®

HR-PP134